RANGER HONOR

TEXAS RANGER HEROES

LYNN SHANNON

Creative Thoughts

Be strong and courageous. Do not be afraid; do not be discouraged, for the Lord your God will be with you wherever you go.

Joshua 1:9

ONE

It was reckless to be driving.

Sheriff Claire Wilson gripped the steering wheel of her patrol truck. Pre-dawn darkness coated the country road, broken only by her headlights. It was below freezing. Last night's thunderstorm had left ice crystals on the trees. The local emergency alert advised people to shelter in place until temperatures rose. Unfortunately, Claire didn't have that luxury. She had a missing person to find.

Using the built-in navigation on her dashboard, Claire dialed Faye Hansen's cell phone. It rang. And rang. Faye didn't answer for the second time in twenty minutes. Her sister—Mary Ellen Hansen—was on a business trip and hadn't been able to reach her sister last night either. Mary Ellen had phoned Claire in the early morning hours, worried.

Her concern was something Claire shared. Faye was one of her best friends. It wasn't like her to ignore phone calls.

Claire pressed the gas pedal as much as she dared. Back roads, like this one, weren't salted. Had Faye been in an accident on her way home from work? It was entirely possible. She co-owned a bakery in town, but lived in a small house near Lake Hudson. Cell service in this area was spotty, and the road was rarely used since there weren't many homes nearby.

Then again, maybe Claire was overreacting. She tended toward worst-case scenarios, an occupational hazard after a decade in law enforcement. Faye's phone could simply be on silent.

Claire's dash lit up with an incoming call. Her heart skipped a beat as she glanced at the name flashing on the screen, but it wasn't Faye. It was Claire's mother.

She answered, using a button on her steering wheel. "Good morning, Mom."

"Morning, honey." Lindsey's voice spilled from the speakers. "I saw your note on the table. I didn't know if you were aware, but there's another wave of rain heading our way. Your daddy's worried about you driving on the icy roads."

Claire nearly smiled. She was closing in on thirty-five and a trained law enforcement officer, but her parents still fretted over her as if she was a child. There had been a time it bothered her. Having her son, Jacob, changed that. Claire was intimately familiar with the constant worry of parenthood. It was like having her heart walking on the outside of her body, packaged in a sweet toddler with curly blond hair and a freckled nose.

"I promised to be extra careful." Claire eyed the sky,

but there was no hint of the sunrise. Probably hidden behind a wall of thunderclouds. "Days like these, the department needs every set of hands. People don't always listen to the weather advisory."

Even without the phone call from Faye's sister, Claire would've been up and out of the house early. Traffic accidents were common when the roads were icy and the incoming thunderstorm made things worse. She sighed. "Call me when Jacob wakes up, would you? I was supposed to be off today. He was looking forward to baking cookies together and now...he's going to be disappointed."

Guilt prickled Claire. As sheriff, her job was mostly administrative. But there were times, like this one, when she needed to be hands-on. As a single mom, it was difficult to balance raising Jacob with a full-time job.

"Don't worry about Jacob, honey. I'll explain you had to go to work. He and I can bake a cake instead. That way he can still help make a dessert and then y'all can bake cookies when you have time off."

"Thanks, Mom."

Claire's thumb absently rubbed over the third finger on her hand. The indention from the wedding ring wasn't there anymore. Not surprising. It'd been two years since her divorce. The marriage hadn't been a happy one, but it'd given Claire the best little boy ever. Moving back home and taking over as sheriff of Fulton County had been a blessing. She was fortunate to have her parents' help in raising Jacob.

She readjusted her hold on the steering wheel. "I'll try to make it home for dinner tonight, but no promises."

"I know. Stay safe, sweetheart. Love you."

Her mother's words came out garbled. Cell coverage in this area was spotty. Claire said "I love you" back, but wasn't sure her mother heard it before the call dropped. Never mind. Claire would call her again later.

The road curved, and she slowed to a crawl. Claire wouldn't be of help to anyone if she was in an accident herself. The tires slipped on black ice but quickly gained traction thanks to her reduced speed. Claire's headlights flashed on a vehicle on the road ahead. An SUV was pulled onto the shoulder, one of the rear tires completely deflated.

Her heart skipped a beat. She knew that car. It belonged to Faye.

Claire flipped on her turret lights and radioed in her location to dispatch before pulling over to the side of the road behind Faye's SUV. Her friend wasn't visible. Maybe she was inside the vehicle, keeping warm. With no cell coverage, it would be impossible to call for a tow truck.

Biting wind ruffled Claire's ponytail as she exited the truck. Goose bumps formed along the delicate skin on the back of her neck. She flipped up the collar of her jacket to ward off the chill. Somewhere, an owl hooted.

"Faye." Claire's boots were silent against the pavement as she rounded the vehicle to the driver's side. "Faye?"

Empty. Faye wasn't in the front seat. Ice covered the

windshield and most of the windows, making it almost impossible to see inside the vehicle.

Claire frowned. Had a neighbor stopped and picked Faye up already? Taken her home? But then why wasn't she answering her cell phone? Dread slithered through Claire's insides, instinctual and hard to explain. Something about this was off. Wrong.

She hurried back to her vehicle. An ice scraper and a flashlight rested in the side panel of her truck. Claire grabbed both.

Claire circled Faye's vehicle, her gaze sweeping the area, following the path of her flashlight. Nothing littered the ground or seemed out of place. She scraped some ice off the driver's side window and shone the light inside the SUV. Faye's purse sat on the floorboard and her cell phone, connected to the charger, rested in the cup holder. The knot of worry and concern inside Claire's stomach grew. Pulling on a set of gloves, she opened the door, touching as little as possible.

She shone the light into the interior of the SUV. Faye wasn't in the back seat. Her wallet was open, the contents spilled across the interior carpeting. The sight heightened Claire's anxiety. She backed away and trailed her flashlight beam along the side of the vehicle. Nothing.

She circled around the front of the vehicle. Her heart stuttered as the beam flashed across the front bumper.

Blood.

It was a dark smear on the chrome. More droplets sprinkled the pavement. Claire followed the trail to the edge of the road. A woman's black ballerina shoe lay on the grass. Another was several feet away. The ditch swelled with rain water. A culvert acted as a makeshift bridge to the forest. Claire ran across, her flashlight beam bouncing with every step. "Faye!"

Silence. Claire scanned the tree line. A short distance away, something pale caught her attention. A bare foot stuck out from the underbrush.

The blood roared in Claire's ears. She wanted to run away. Duty and a sliver of hope kept her moving forward. *Please, Lord. Please don't let it be true.*

Grass crunched under Claire's boots. A biting chill that had nothing to do with the frigid weather settled over her. Into her. The flashlight passed over the woman's chest. Blood stained the blouse. A lot of blood. Too much blood.

"Faye!" Claire bolted to her friend's side and dropped to her knees. Icy water seeped through the fabric of her uniform, but she barely felt it. She tore one of her gloves off. It fell to the ground. Faye's skin was as pale as snow, her eyes closed. If she was breathing, it wasn't evident.

With shaking fingers, tears streaming unbidden down her face, Claire reached a trembling hand toward Faye's neck, praying with every cell in her body that she'd find a pulse.

TWO

Texas Ranger Gavin Sterling guzzled the last of his coffee before shoving open his truck door. Bitterly cold wind stole his breath. He zipped his heavy jacket then settled his Stetson on his head. Yellow crime scene tape fluttered across several tree branches. A coroner's van was parked between two Fulton County Sheriff patrol cars. Swollen, dark clouds overhead promised more rain.

It was a miserable day to be at a crime scene, but Gavin hadn't joined law enforcement to sit behind a desk. Someone had been murdered. It was his job to find the killer and get justice.

He spotted Sheriff Claire Wilson and headed in her direction. Gavin had met the sheriff at a fellow ranger's wedding last week. The petite blond had knocked his socks off in a beautiful silk dress that brought out the crystal blue color of her eyes, but they hadn't gotten further than brief introductions. Claire had ducked out of the reception early.

Today, she was wearing a heavy jacket with the word sheriff written on the back. Her shoulder-length hair was pulled into a low ponytail. Mud coated her shoes. She was staring at the tree line with a look Gavin couldn't quite place. Sensing his approach, she turned. Claire's eyes were red-rimmed, as if she was on the verge of crying.

Gavin's heart sank. He recognized the pain etched on her expression before she smoothed it out. Claire had known the victim. Probably well. It might even be a relative.

"Ranger Sterling, thank you for coming so quickly." Claire cleared her throat and extended a hand. "Especially since you drove across two counties in awful weather to get here."

Gavin didn't normally work in Fulton County. His friend and colleague, Bennett Knox, handled this area. But Bennett and his new wife, Emilia, were currently on their honeymoon after their wedding last week—the same wedding Claire and Gavin had first met at. Claire had been a bridesmaid. She'd been instrumental in taking down a serial killer last year and, as a result, had forged a close friendship with Emilia.

"No need to thank me, Sheriff." Gavin slipped his hand into hers. Claire's grip was firm, her skin silky. He ignored the jolt of attraction coursing up his arm. As the newest member of Company A, Gavin had no desire to mix his personal life with his professional one. "I'm glad to assist in any way I can. And you can call me Gavin."

She nodded. "Claire, then."

Gavin dropped her hand. He jerked his chin toward the crime scene tape. "What can you tell me?"

"The victim is thirty-five-year-old Faye Hansen." Claire met his eyes. "She was one of my best friends. Which brings me to my first order of business. You won't be just assisting with this case. You'll be the lead investigator."

"I don't mind being in charge, but..." He tilted his head, studying her. "Why hand the case to me?"

"I can't guarantee my objectivity. As I said before, Faye and I were close. When we catch the monster who did this—and we will catch him—I don't want a defense attorney using my relationship with the victim against us in court. This case has to be rock solid."

Gavin's esteem for Claire as a law enforcement officer went up several notches. Handing over control of a case wasn't common. It was clear her focus was on getting justice, not the credit. Bennett said Claire was one of the best he'd ever worked with. Gavin understood why and he'd only been with her for three minutes.

He nodded sharply. "Understood. And on a personal note, I'm sorry for your loss."

"Thank you." She took a deep breath and squared her shoulders before leading him further into the crime scene. "Okay, as I said, the victim is Faye Hansen. Caucasian. Single, no children. Her sister, Mary Ellen, called me personally this morning because she hadn't been able to reach Faye since yesterday evening."

"I take it that was out-of-the-ordinary?"

"Extremely. Faye and Mary Ellen own a bakery in

town together. They talk and text numerous times per day." Claire gestured up the road. "Faye lives about five miles that way. This is the route she normally takes to get home. And this is her SUV."

The vehicle was parked on the side of the road. One rear tire was flat. Gavin bent down to inspect the rubber more closely. His heart skipped a beat. "This tire appears to have been slashed." He removed a pair of latex gloves from his pocket and pulled them on. Then he ran a finger along the jagged edge of the cut. "It's not wide enough to have flattened the tire immediately."

Claire's mouth tightened. "No. My guess is the killer did it to force Faye to pull over in a secluded area."

His gaze narrowed. "She was targeted. Do you know why?"

"No, but the killer wanted us to believe the motive was robbery. Faye closed the bakery last night, and it was her habit to take the cash and receipts home. She did the accounting and then deposited the funds in the bank the next morning. The money is missing."

"How much are we talking about?"

"Roughly five hundred dollars. People have killed for less, but slashing Faye's tire seems like an unnecessary step. If the killer was merely after the money, he could've robbed her in the parking lot." Claire opened the driver's side door. "Faye's purse is still here. Her wallet was rifled through, but the killer didn't take the twenty dollars inside. And Faye's expensive cell phone is still in the cup holder."

A quick inspection of the interior confirmed Claire's

observations. Why would a thief take the bakery's cash, but leave Faye's? And the cell phone was easy pickings. Something about this was definitely off. "Could Faye have stopped somewhere on her way home?"

"Unlikely. Witnesses reported seeing her leave the bakery around nine last night. I have the passcode to Faye's phone and accessed her call log. She attempted to call roadside assistance at 9:20 several times, but this stretch of road has terrible cell service. I don't think the calls ever went through."

Claire circled the front of the SUV, her stride strong and purposefully. She pointed to a muddy indentation on the side of the road. Tire tracks. "The killer stopped his vehicle here. Faye must've known the person because she got out of her SUV. Probably thinking the person was going to help her. Instead, he shot her."

Blood spattered the chrome bumper of Faye's SUV, supporting Claire's theory. Gavin's gaze drifted to the activity near the tree line. Two men from the coroner's office attended to the body. A woman's shoe lay in the grass.

Gavin's gut clenched as his mind filled in the blanks. "Faye tried to escape."

"Yes." Claire led the way to the body. "But the killer shot her twice more in the back as she ran away."

Faye was resting on her stomach. Her long dark hair was tangled and wet from the rain. Blood stained the grass around her body, as well as her white blouse. She'd been terrified, running for her life, when the killer hunted her down like an animal. It was cruel.

Anger raised Gavin's body temperature until it felt like he was boiling inside his jacket. He hadn't known Faye Hansen in life, but she was a part of him now. And he wouldn't stop until her killer was behind bars.

Gavin drew in a breath. The cold air hurt his lungs, and when he let it out slowly, condensation hung in the air. His gaze swept across the crime scene.

Claire tilted her head. "What are you thinking?"

"That you're right. This wasn't a robbery. Taking the money was an afterthought, a way to throw us off the real reason she was murdered. Do you have any idea who may have done this?"

"None. Faye is..." She struggled for a moment before clearing her throat. "She was well-loved by everyone. It sounds cliche, but she didn't have any enemies."

"She had one. Whoever did this is someone Faye knew. She got out of her SUV when the killer drove up. She wasn't afraid." His gaze swept the crime scene again before settling back on Claire. She needed to be prepared for what may come next. "This killer...it's a neighbor. A friend. Since you and Faye were close—"

"It may be someone I care deeply about." Claire's voice was hollow, but she held his gaze. "I know that, Gavin. Like I said before, I can't trust my objectivity regarding this case. That's why you're here."

Fulton County had two bakeries. One was closer to the freeway and frequented by travelers looking for a quick bite. Sadly, it'd been linked to the serial killer case Claire worked last year. An employee had been nabbed from the parking lot during the early morning hours. She survived the encounter with the murderer, thankfully, and was currently in college.

Now, the town's second pastry shop was a crime scene. Sweets and Treats Bakery was nestled between a laundromat and an antique store. Dripping icicles hung from the striped awning. Graceful letters written in Faye's artistic scrawl announced the house special: a coffee and cinnamon bun combo. Claire's throat tightened at the sight of the familiar establishment. She would never again cross the threshold and see her friend's bright smile greeting her from across the counter. Faye was gone. Tears pricked Claire's eyes.

Don't think about it. She sucked in a breath. There would be time to grieve for Faye, but it wasn't now. Claire's job was to get justice. She released her iron grip on the steering wheel and exited her patrol truck. Gavin's official state vehicle pulled into the parking spot next to hers. His dark hair was shorn on the sides and top, but the rigid hairstyle suited the sharp planes of his face. A full mouth was softened the deep cleft in his chin. The chestnut-colored blazer encasing his broad shoulders matched his eyes. This was her second time meeting Gavin, and her impression was exactly the same. The man was distractingly handsome. It was a fact she was determined to ignore. Claire had enough problems on her plate without adding romance to the mix. She had a town to protect and a son to raise.

A killer to catch.

Turning the case over to a complete stranger wasn't easy. Trust didn't come easily to Claire anymore. A side effect of her failed marriage, perhaps, or simply a jaded outlook from a career in law enforcement. But she was smart enough to recognize the dangers of working Faye's murder investigation herself. It wasn't possible. Already she was struggling to keep the grief at bay. Claire wouldn't dishonor her friend by mucking up the case.

She had to trust someone. Gavin's reputation as a Texas Ranger was far-reaching. He closed most of his cases because of a solid work ethic and a dogged determination. Additionally, as an outsider, he'd be able to see townsfolk for who they were and not with the skewed perception that often plagued her subordinates. No one wanted to believe their friend or neighbor was a killer. Not even Claire's deputies.

"Beautiful town." Gavin joined her on the sidewalk. He hit a button on his fob, causing a subsequent beep from his truck as the locks engaged. "Did you grow up here?"

He was a head taller than her and, coupled with his muscular frame, made Claire feel surprisingly dainty. Feminine. It was unsettling. Dangerous akin to attraction. She took a step away from him. "Yes, I grew up here. My parents own rental cabins along Lake Hudson. Winter is quiet, but in spring and summer, Fulton County gets a lot of tourists. Professional fisherman, families, that kind of thing."

Gavin waved a finger at the nearby businesses. "Any of them have surveillance cameras?"

"No. And honestly, there isn't much need for them. Our crime rate is extremely low. Faye's murder, the serial killer we caught last year...those were anomalies. I took over as sheriff last year and most of my days are spent dealing with partying teenagers and minor traffic accidents." She jutted her thumb over her shoulder. "Faye parked around back. Mind the ice on the walkway."

Gavin fell into step beside her. His stride was confident and easy. "What did you do before becoming sheriff?"

"I spent ten years as an agent with the FBI."

He whistled. "This job must be a big change of pace for you then."

"It is, but I needed it." She paused, uncertain how much to share, but quickly dismissed the silly feeling. Gavin was going to be in town for a while and gossip ran faster in Fulton County than the internet. He'd hear about her past from someone. Better it came from her. "I have a three-year-old son named Jacob. It's a long story, but his father and I divorced shortly after he was born. Staying in the FBI, working the kinds of hours I was, wasn't possible as a single-mother. When the sheriff's position opened up, I jumped at it. My parents watch Jacob for me while I'm working."

"I'm sorry to hear about your divorce. It's far too common in our line of work."

She slid a glance in his direction. "Are you speaking from experience?"

"No. I never made it to the altar." He was quiet for a long moment. A shadow crossed his face. "I got close once though."

There was a layer of pain in his voice that touched her, but she instinctively knew Gavin didn't want to share more. Fair enough. After all, they barely knew one another. Or maybe speaking the words was too painful. That was a feeling she was intimately familiar with.

Claire's foot hit a piece of ice and she tipped backward. Gavin's hand shot out, firmly gripping her elbow and stopping her fall. Her heart skipped a beat. His dark eyes had golden flecks, and the scent of his aftershave—woodsy and clean—tickled her senses. She sucked in a breath. "Oops. Thanks."

His mouth curved at the corners, sending her heart rate into overdrive. "Anytime, Claire."

There was something about the way he said her name. And when Gavin dropped his hand from her elbow, she felt a pang of loss. Ridiculous. What on earth was wrong with her? Claire wasn't the moony type. Had never been. Then again, her best friend had been murdered. It was far easier to focus on the handsome Texas Ranger than on the case.

Claire took another breath of cold air, letting it ice her lungs and hopefully re-engage her common sense. She turned the corner of the building. The rear of the bakery sported two parking spots and a dumpster. An alley connected the space to a side street. "This is where Faye parked her car. As I said earlier, witnesses reported seeing her leave the bakery around nine last night."

Gavin turned in a circle, a frown marring his handsome features. He pointed to the lights on the rear of the bakery. "How bright are those?"

"Minimal. The killer could've slipped back here and sliced Faye's tire without being seen. The bakery doesn't have cameras in this area. There is one inside the store, but it's focused on the cash register."

"That's...unhelpful." His frown deepened. "We should look at the video from last night, anyway. Maybe the killer went into the bakery before coming back here to sabotage Faye's car."

"It's a thought. Faye's sister, Mary Ellen, canceled the rest of her business trip. She's driving straight to the sheriff's department. I'll call my chief deputy to see if Mary Ellen has arrived." Claire removed her phone from her jacket pocket, but the device tumbled from her numb fingers. The freezing temperatures weren't doing her any favors. Thankfully, the phone had a virtually indestructible waterproof case. She swept down to retrieve it.

Something whizzed over her head. Glass shattered as a rear window on the bakery exploded. Gavin slammed into Claire and they tumbled to the ground in a mass of arms and legs. The air whooshed from her lungs, but her mind had already put the pieces together.

Someone was shooting at them.

THREE

They were exposed.

Embedded instinct took over as Gavin cradled Claire's head in the crook of his neck and rolled, shifting them behind the protective cover of the dumpster. The Taser on her duty belt jabbed his stomach. Cold liquid seeped into the sleeve of his blazer. He barely felt it. His only concern was Claire. Had she been hit?

Gavin released her, his gaze sweeping over her slender form. A small scrape marred the delicate curve of her cheek and she looked furious enough to spit nails but otherwise appeared unharmed. Relief unclamped his stomach, but the reprieve was brief. More glass on the bakery windows shattered, followed by pings on the metal dumpster as the shooter sprayed them. Several bullets pounded into the wooden fence behind Gavin. He pulled his gun.

Claire reached for her weapon, sliding closer to the

dumpster's side. She held her cell in the other hand. "Where is he?"

"I'm not sure." Gavin peeked around the corner of the dumpster. There was only one building tall enough with a clear line of sight. "Is that a hospital? Second floor. The one under construction."

More bullets slammed into the metal, this time much closer to their position. Gavin slunk lower. He prayed the dumpster would be strong enough to absorb the bullets. There was always a risk one would pass through and hit one of them.

"It's not a hospital. It's an emergency clinic." Claire relayed their position and situation to dispatch in clipped tones. Then she hung up. "Backup is on the way, but the shooter will bolt before they get here. I'm going after him."

"We're going after him," Gavin corrected. Staying put wasn't an option. The shooter had fired on two law enforcement officers in the broad light of day. Chances were, this attack was connected to Faye's murder. A criminal that determined and dangerous had to be caught.

Claire met his gaze for a heartbeat and nodded sharply. "Follow me."

She shifted into a crouch. A straw wrapper was snagged in the silky strands of her blond hair and her previously pressed and perfect uniform was stained. But her expression...it was captivating. Focused. Determined. Driven.

Beautiful.

It was a wayward thought Gavin didn't have a second

to process. Adrenaline narrowed his focus as he sprang from behind the dumpster and followed Claire down the small alley to the side street. The edge of his cowboy boot hit a patch of ice. His foot slid, threatening to upend him, but he caught himself at the last moment. He added more fuel to his legs, joining Claire at the entrance of the emergency clinic.

The automatic doors slid open with a whoosh. Several people were sitting in the waiting room and a nurse stood blocking the path to the interior exam rooms. Her eyes widened at the sight of their drawn weapons.

Gavin didn't slow down. "Where's the stairwell leading to the upper floor?"

The nurse blinked. "It's closed—"

"Stairwell," Claire commanded. Her tone was sharp and her feet never stopped moving as she brushed past the nurse. Gavin stayed on her heels. The nurse pointed to the left, and they took off down the hall. The door leading to the second floor was unlocked.

Gavin grabbed Claire's arm before she could ascend the stairs. He leaned in closer to her ear. "Let me go first."

She looked like she wanted to argue for a moment, but then acquiesced. Another mark in the plus column in Gavin's book. Claire wasn't reckless or unwilling to be a team player. The shooter had been aiming for her. She was his target. The criminal could be lying in wait, hoping for Claire to appear first so he could take her out.

Gavin wouldn't give him the chance.

Claire stepped back, allowing Gavin to slip past her. The stairwell was concrete. He lightened his steps to prevent his boots from making any noise. Nerves jittered his stomach as he turned the corner on the landing, but the hand holding his weapon was steady. Claire matched him step for step. Her presence was both a comfort and a responsibility.

There was no door separating the stairs from the upper level. This was the riskiest part. In order to ascend, Gavin's head would be exposed before the rest of his body. He pressed himself against the wall and the railing shoved against the small of his back. His heart rate increased. Gavin took deep breaths to counteract his narrowing vision. He paused on the stairs, straining to listen for any sound in the floor above them.

Nothing.

Sweat dripped down Gavin's back. He inhaled once more and then took the stairs two at a time, letting his gaze sweep across the space for any sign of color or movement. Behind him, Claire followed. As he swept left, she went right. Training made them a good team. Nails and dust littered the floor. Metal framing delineated future rooms, but the sheet rock hadn't been placed yet. A wash of frigid air blew into the space from an open window.

The shooter was gone.

An hour later, Claire dabbed antiseptic on a nasty cut along her calf. A pounding headache made her stomach churn. Her body was bruised from the hard impact with the concrete and her uniform smelled like sour icing. But she was alive.

Thank you, God. The last thing I want to do is leave Jacob without a mother.

She was a law enforcement officer. A professional. Risking her life came with the badge, but motherhood had placed an additional responsibility on her shoulders. One she was still struggling to balance with her career. Days like today brought that point home in a raw way.

Claire had made her fair share of enemies. Every law enforcement officer did. But this morning's shooting, coming on the heels of Faye's murder, couldn't be random. The two incidents had to be connected. Gavin believed Claire was the true target since the initial shot had been aimed at her. But why? What purpose did the killer hope to gain by killing her? It would only draw more attention to the case.

None of it made sense. Hopefully, Faye's sister, Mary Ellen, could provide some insight.

Claire ripped open a bandage and applied it to her calf. She splashed cold water on her face, redid her ponytail, and then squared her shoulders. Everyone—including her subordinates—would be watching her. She had to set the right example. Calm, cool, and collected.

Even if a murderer had her in his sights.

Claire exited the bathroom. The sounds of the phones ringing and voices drifted down the hall from the deputies' area. Her cell phone, tucked in her pocket, vibrated. She pulled it out and groaned at the name written across the screen.

Mayor Patrick Scott.

He was calling about the case. She pictured him sitting in his office at City Hall, the heavy drapery on the large windows behind him, several members of his staff hovering around like bees. Patrick was well-liked, but Claire found him pretentious and more concerned with his reputation than doing the right thing.

Drawing from a well of patience, Claire accepted the call. "Good morning, Mayor."

"Sheriff, finally. I've called the department three times and no one could locate you. The media are clamoring for a comment about the bakery shooting. We need to get the story right, otherwise it'll be a mess. What do you know? Do you have suspects?"

It didn't escape Claire's notice that Patrick didn't waste his breath asking if she was okay. She tamped down her frustration with him. One of the good things about Patrick was his ability to handle the media. It kept them off her back. She was very grateful for that.

Claire quickly ran through what they knew. When she finished, Patrick was so quiet she thought the call had dropped. "Sir?"

"Sorry, I'm thinking. This case isn't like any other. The media attention is going to be on us, much like it was last year with the serial killer. I want complete updates from you every three hours. If there's a major break in the investigation, I need to know immediately."

"Every three hours may be difficult, sir, but I promise to keep you abreast of the situation."

"Not good enough, Sheriff. I don't need to tell you

what a critical time this is. Elections are around the corner. People will be watching us."

Claire didn't care a fig about the election. Her goal was to obtain justice for Faye and protect the citizens of her county. If she didn't do that, then she didn't deserve to be sheriff. "You have my word, sir. I will do everything in my power to catch the criminal behind this and put him behind bars."

She hung up. The pounding in her head was increasing exponentially. Claire turned the corner and nearly ran into Gavin standing outside her office. He'd shed his sports jacket and the ranger badge pinned to the front pocket of his shirt shone in the fluorescent lighting. For a moment, the feeling of his arms wrapped around her as they rolled behind the dumpster flashed in Claire's mind. His touch had been gentle and tender, despite the dangerous circumstances.

She shoved the errant thought from her mind. Her focus needed to be on the case. "Ready to talk to Mary Ellen?"

"Yep. She's waiting for us inside the interview room." He lifted his hand. A small packet of over-the-counter painkillers rested in his palm. "I took some already. Figured you might need them too."

The gesture was thoughtful and kind. It caught Claire off-guard. She wasn't used to being taken care of by anyone other than her parents. Her gaze narrowed as she plucked the pills from his palm. "You aren't going to ask if I want to go home, are you?"

His mouth quirked. "I wouldn't dream of it. I already know you'd refuse."

Claire accepted the bottle of water Gavin offered and downed the pills. "Thank you. And thanks for having my back this morning."

The mirth fled from his expression. He pointed to the cross discreetly pinned to her uniform shirt. "You're a believer?"

"I am."

"Then you'll understand this when I say, God brought me here. He used me as an instrument to protect you. I'm glad He did, Claire, and I promise to do everything in my power to solve this case."

The man kept surprising her. His insightful words clicked open something inside her heart. She might not want to pursue this attraction to Gavin, but she would be fortunate to have his friendship.

Before she could say anything, Gavin continued, "I'd like your permission to have state troopers increase patrols near your family's home. As a precautionary measure. Just until we know what we're dealing with."

He was worried the shooter might use Claire's family as a means to get to her. She'd already considered that. It didn't seem likely, but she wouldn't take any chances. Not when it came to the people she loved most in the world. "Do it. I've already asked my own deputies to increase patrols, but every set of extra eyes helps. I've also spoken with my father and explained the situation. Dad has a home security system. He's also an expert marksman."

Gavin nodded. "I've met your father. Took a Sports and Wilderness First Aid training course from him. He's good at what he does."

"He is." Pride swelled in her chest. Her parents had worked hard to build their wilderness and cabin rental business from scratch. Claire's younger sister, Bea, would take over next year. She was currently attending a seminar in Denver. "Come on. Let's not leave Mary Ellen waiting any longer."

Claire and Gavin walked to the interview room. Mary Ellen stood when they entered. Late-thirties, she was older than Faye by five years. Her dark hair was tucked into a messy bun and she'd dressed in sweats. Her eyes were red-rimmed and swollen from crying. Several crumpled tissues lay on the table.

A deputy—one of Claire's best—had been assigned to wait with Mary Ellen and comfort her. He nodded in Claire's direction before leaving the room, closing the door gently behind him.

Mary Ellen rushed forward. "Claire, thank God. Are you okay? I overheard them saying you'd been shot. The deputy wouldn't tell me anything, no matter how many times I asked."

Claire embraced the other woman. "He's not allowed to speak about an ongoing case. Don't be angry with him." She pulled back, holding on to Mary Ellen's arm. Her complexion was paler than the ice crystals hanging outside the window. "Thank you for driving straight here. Can I get you anything? Coffee or water?"

"No. Nothing."

"Did the deputy offer to call your husband for you?"

She nodded. "Pete's in Alaska on a business trip, and my kids are staying with their grandparents. I've already spoken to my aunt. She's driving up to stay with me until they get here."

Mary Ellen's gaze shot to Gavin. Claire made introductions and explained his role in the investigation. Then they all sat at the conference table. Mary Ellen grabbed a new tissue and swiped at the tears leaking from her eyes. "I'm sorry. I can't stop crying. After you called and told me about Faye, I focused on getting here. But once I got into this room... it gave me time to think."

Her grief was palpable, and it took everything inside Claire to keep her own under control. She reached across the table and squeezed the other woman's hand. "Cry as much as you want, Mary Ellen. We'll take this one step at a time."

"No. I can do this." She took a shaky breath. "There's something you need to know, Claire. Faye was looking into a missing person's case from two years ago. Stephanie Madden. She worked for us at the bakery."

Shock reverberated through Claire. Two years ago, she hadn't been sheriff. Her predecessor—Randy King—had been in charge then. Dread circled her insides. Sheriff King, as the townspeople still called him, had often made mistakes while investigating cases. Faye had mentioned Stephanie in passing to Claire, but never said the woman was missing. "I thought Stephanie left town."

"That's what Sheriff King told us. But Faye never believed it. She had a fondness for Stephanie, had

27

mentored her through high school and after graduation. She even rented my grandmother's cottage to her at a discounted rate. When she supposedly left town, Stephanie was working for us and attending community college. She was responsible and hardworking. Faye found it difficult to believe Stephanie would simply pack up and leave town without saying something first."

"Why didn't Faye come to me about it?"

Mary Ellen sighed. "She intended to, but Stephanie's family claims she's living in Houston. Faye didn't want to bother you if that was true. She hired a private investigator and asked him to search for Stephanie."

Beside her, Gavin scribbled notes on his pad. "Do you know the name of the private investigator?"

"Michael Grayson. Faye called me last night from the store while she was closing up and said that she'd gotten some news from him. We were supposed to discuss it later in the evening when she got home..." Mary Ellen's eyes swam with fresh tears as a sob cut off her sentence.

Faye had never made it home.

FOUR

Gavin scowled at the image displayed on the computer screen. It was a closeup of the shooter taken from the emergency clinic's surveillance video. The man was dressed in all black, a ski cap pulled low on his head. A backpack—big enough to hide a disassembled rifle—was slung over one shoulder.

"Is this the best image we have of him?" Gavin asked.

"I'm afraid so, sir." Keith O'Neal, Claire's chief deputy, swiped a hand over his ginger mustache. Pushing fifty, he had the physique of a much younger man, but the lines on his face told of long hours and troublesome cases. Gavin had worked with Keith years ago, when he was with the Houston Police Department. Drug abuse had derailed his career for a time. Gavin was happy to see him sober. Keith was one of the good ones.

Gavin turned to Claire. She was studying the image on the computer screen. Stains from hiding behind the dumpster marred her uniform, but she'd scraped her hair into a fresh ponytail. A butterfly bandage covered the scratch on her cheek. On the credenza behind her were several photographs. Most of them featured a smiling toddler with golden hair and sweet freckles. Her son, Jacob. He resembled his mother.

The photographs of Claire and her young child were physical reminders of the responsibility weighing on Gavin's shoulders. A part of him wanted to seclude Claire and her family away. But that wasn't fair. Nor was it possible. Claire was the sheriff and had a job to do. Gavin respected that.

The glow from the computer screen caressed Claire's features. Taken apart, one by one, they were too different to be considered classically pretty. A wide mouth, sharply cut jaw, high forehead, and the faint freckles sprinkled on her nose. But joined together, there was something captivating about them...

Gavin wrangled his runaway thoughts from Claire's beauty. Yes, she was gorgeous. And he'd been impressed with the way she handled the shooting. But this attraction couldn't go any further. Gavin's relationship with Claire was professional, and that's exactly how it would stay.

Claire frowned. "Play the video again from the beginning, Keith."

Her chief deputy complied. The shooter slipped out of a side door and skirted the edge of the building before disappearing down an alley. Claire shook her head. "He could be anyone."

Keith made a grunt of agreement. "I think that was

the point." Worry tightened the lines on his forehead as he closed his laptop. "Did you find Stephanie Madden's case file in the storage room?"

"Yep." Claire picked up a file folder from her desk and pushed it toward him. "There's not much to it. Mary Ellen was correct. Sheriff King determined Stephanie simply left town."

Gavin had also read the case file. Two years ago, Stephanie was reported missing by her boss, Faye. Deputies knocked on her door, but she didn't answer, and her car wasn't in the driveway. After a few days, when Stephanie didn't reappear, a search warrant was obtained for her home. A suitcase was missing, as were clothes and other personal items.

"I've searched for Stephanie in the databases," Gavin said. "Nothing shows up. Her driver's license expired and she hasn't renewed it. Her car's yearly registration is out-of-date. No arrests. No updated address."

Claire's jaw tightened. "Considering Faye's murder, that doesn't bode well for us. I'm not sure we're going to find Stephanie alive."

Gavin picked up a photograph of Stephanie, taken from her case file. She was a beautiful blonde with a sunny smile. He wanted to believe she was out there, somewhere, living her life. But he was afraid Claire was right. Stephanie was likely dead.

He rose from the chair and strolled to the whiteboard attached to a standing easel. Using a magnet, he stuck Stephanie's photograph next to the ones from Faye's crime scene. His gaze swept across the images.

"Let's go through what we know so far, starting with Faye."

Keith nodded, flipping to a page in his notebook. "She worked all day at the bakery. Witnesses I've interviewed said she was in a good mood, nothing out of the ordinary. Faye mentioned to her last customer that she was meeting someone after closing. She didn't say who. The camera over the register was turned off at 8:41."

Gavin tapped a photograph of Faye's slashed tire. "Maybe she met with her attacker? We know Faye was looking into Stephanie's disappearance. She could've mentioned it to the wrong person."

"That makes sense." Claire began pacing. "Okay, Faye meets with someone about Stephanie. Whatever is said causes the killer to walk out of the bakery and puncture Faye's tire."

"Why not kill her inside the bakery?" Keith interjected. His feet were propped up on the conference table and he spun a pen between his fingers. "It would've been a lot easier."

"Maybe the killer was worried about potential witnesses. Or maybe he didn't have his gun with him inside the bakery. We can't assume the killer knew what the conversation was going to be about when he arrived to meet with Faye. She may have caught him off-guard." Claire pointed to the slice on the tire. "This cut could've been made with a strong pocket knife. People regularly carry them. It would've been easy to stab the tire after leaving the bakery and then follow Faye home, waiting for her to get a flat tire."

Gavin envisioned the crime in his mind's eye. "Faye pulls to the side of the road. She tries calling for roadside assistance, but can't get through. The killer drives up. Faye gets out."

He could imagine the exchange. The pleasantries and relief on Faye's part. The trust she must've had...until the moment the killer pulled out a gun. It made Gavin's heart ache. "After shooting Faye, the killer goes to her SUV. He takes the cash from the store, hoping we'll think it's a robbery gone wrong."

Claire nodded. "Except we figure out Faye's murder is connected to Stephanie's disappearance."

"That's why you're a target, Sheriff." Keith sat up, his feet thudding against the floor as they dropped from the conference table. "Your replacement could classify Faye's murder as a robbery gone south and then say Stephanie's disappearance is unrelated. People here are used to Sheriff King's way of doing things."

Gavin had never worked with the former sheriff of Fulton County personally, but he'd heard the rumors. Sheriff King let his personal relationships with people influence his investigations. With disastrous results. A serial killer had been overlooked and murdered several more women before Claire finally closed the case. And that was only one example. Gavin knew there were more. Stephanie's flimsy case file was proof enough that Sheriff King hadn't investigated her disappearance thoroughly.

"I hate to say it, but I think Keith is on to something." Gavin rocked back on his heels. "I'm here because of your invitation. Texas Rangers don't have jurisdiction over local murders or disappearances. The next sheriff could ask me to leave and close these cases as he sees fit."

Gavin didn't have hard evidence of the killer's motives, but his gut said they were on the right track. Which meant Claire was still in danger. The killer would keep coming after her. The thought made Gavin's blood boil. He wouldn't allow anyone to harm her. Not on his watch.

Claire scowled. "If you're right, and the killer is attempting to get rid of me to avoid these cases being investigated thoroughly, then I'm very concerned about the private investigator Faye hired. Michael Grayson could answer a lot of our questions. Have we been able to track him down yet?"

Gavin shared her fear. "He hasn't been seen since last night. My colleague, Ranger Weston Donovan, is searching for him. We've listing him as a critical missing."

Every officer in the state was looking for the man. Claire sighed, rubbing her forehead as if her head was still bothering her. "We need to find him."

"Agreed. We're doing all we can." Gavin leaned back in his chair. He studied a photograph of the shooter extracted from the surveillance video. Frustration bubbled at the blurriness of the criminal's face. "We need to focus our attention on Stephanie's disappearance. Figuring out what happened to her should lead us to Faye's killer since the two cases are linked."

Claire nodded. "Let's start by talking to Stephanie's mom. I'd like to find out what she knows about her daughter living in Houston."

"Careful, Sheriff." Keith's tone was ominous. "Stephanie's stepfather, Xavier Whitlock, doesn't like law enforcement."

She grimaced. "I know."

Claire kept both hands on the steering wheel while driving to the Whitlock property. She had all-weather tires, but the temperature hadn't risen above freezing all day. Black ice was a treacherous prospect. Dark clouds hovering beyond the windshield promised even more heavy rain. The two-lane country road was empty. Most of the people were hunkered down, waiting for the storm to pass.

"Why doesn't Xavier Whitlock like law enforcement?" Gavin asked from the passenger seat. His long legs were tucked under the dash and his cowboy hat rested in his lap. He tapped on his phone screen. "I've reviewed his criminal record. He's been arrested a few times for misdemeanor assaults, but the cases are over twenty years old. There's nothing recent."

"He's a survivalist." Claire flipped on her wipers to combat the drizzle sprinkling the glass. "Xavier is part of a group known as the Chosen."

Gavin inhaled sharply. "They've been on our radar for a long time. Paramilitary, known to stock-pile weapons and suspected of drug trafficking."

"Now you know why he doesn't like law enforcement. Xavier claims he only follows the policies of the

Chosen. Living independently, off the grid, that kind of thing. And, to be honest, it could be true. We've kept our eye on him and never caught Xavier doing anything illegal. On the other hand, the property he owns is vast. Over 200 acres, much of it wooded."

"So it would be easy for him to hide illegal activity." A muscle in Gavin's powerful jaw twitched. "If something did happen to Stephanie, her stepfather could have motive. Maybe she knew something about him. Threatened to tell law enforcement."

"It's not out of the realm of possibility." Claire turned onto a dirt road leading to the Whitlock house. The rain had turned it into a mud pit. She hit the brakes, eying the large puddles coated with a sheen of ice. The last thing she wanted was to be stuck on the Whitlock property waiting on a tow-truck. Especially in this weather. "Sorry, but I think we should walk the rest of the way to the house."

Gavin nodded. Claire zipped up her coat and exited the vehicle. Her boots sank into the muck. She snagged her own cowboy hat from the rear to keep the drizzle off her face, but the frigid air, so unusual for a Texas winter, shocked her lungs.

"How far is the house?" Gavin asked. His gaze swept over the tree-lined path. Shadows lurked, big enough to hide a person in. Claire could feel the tension in his body. The hair on the back of her neck rose. It felt like they were being watched.

"The house is about 50 yards ahead of us." Claire stepped closer to Gavin until they were shoulder to shoulder. She lowered her voice, so it wouldn't carry on the wind. "Xavier isn't stupid. Even if he is the one behind Faye's murder and the shooting this morning, he's not going to attack us while we're on his property. It would draw too much attention."

Gavin met her gaze. This close, she could see the specks of green and gold buried in his warm brown eyes. Butterflies fluttered in her stomach when the corner of his mouth hitched upward. "Xavier may think twice about hurting us, but stick close to me all the same, would you?"

She nodded, tearing her gaze from his. She needed to do a better job of ignoring this annoying hum of attraction between them. It could only cause trouble.

They maneuvered past a large puddle. Rain pattered against the tree leaves. It was colder in the shelter of the woods. Claire's breath came in puffs that hung in the air. Gavin stayed close to her side, one hand on the holster of his weapon, as they followed the road to the house.

Something rustled in the trees ahead of them. Claire halted. Her gaze swept the tree line. "Who's there?"

Xavier stepped out of the tree line. A long beard covered the lower half of his face and a ski cap hid his hair. He wore a camouflage jacket, cargo pants, and military-style boots. A rifle rested in his hands, barrel pointed upward. "You're trespassing on my land."

Claire stepped forward. "I need to speak to your wife, Xavier. It's police business."

"What kind of business do you have with Maribelle?"

"It's about your stepdaughter, Stephanie."

No flicker of surprise crossed Xavier's face. Claire's muscles tightened with tension. The video of the shooter they had was grainy and of poor quality, but Xavier was the right height and weight. The rifle in his hands was a high-powered one, similar to the make and model used by the shooter this morning.

Circumstantial evidence. But it left her with questions. Was Gavin right? Was she looking at a killer?

"Stephanie hasn't been around for a long time, Sheriff. No need to go looking for her now." Xavier's expression darkened. "That girl's a troublemaker, anyway. I guarantee, you'll only find problems where she's concerned."

Was that a threat? It certainly seemed like one.

"Be that as it may, I have a job to do." Claire jutted up her chin in a challenge. "I need to speak to your wife. If you have nothing to hide, then it's better to answer my questions."

Xavier's scowl deepened. For a long moment, Claire wasn't sure the man would let them pass. Then he turned and started up the road. "Let's make it quick, Sheriff. I don't like visitors."

Claire glanced at Gavin. He'd remained silent during the entire exchange, but his hand still rested on his weapon holster. There was a fierce expression on his face. No wonder Xavier didn't argue further.

The trees parted and a small farmhouse came into view. The front porch was swept clean, the siding freshly painted. Flower beds neatly outlined with bricks held trimmed bushes. Several plants were covered to protect them from the cold with white sheets. Clothes lines, hung between two poles, stood empty.

"Maribelle," Xavier shouted. "Come out here. The sheriff wants a word."

The screen door creaked as a woman stepped onto the porch. Her dark hair was threaded with gray and a washed-out dress hung on her slender frame. She didn't have a coat on. Claire surmised a stiff wind could knock her over. Maribelle had lost a lot of weight in the last year. Was she ill? Or did they not have enough food? Xavier wasn't the type to reach out for help if it was the latter.

Claire nodded in greeting. "Mrs. Sterling, I'm here to ask about your daughter, Stephanie. Have you heard from her recently?"

Maribelle crossed her arms over her midsection. If Claire's question surprised her, it didn't show in her expression. "No, ma'am."

"When was the last time you spoke to her?"

"I don't recall. She's living in Houston now. I got a postcard from her a while back, letting me know she was okay."

"Do you have the postcard? Could I see it?"

Maribelle passed a glance toward her husband and he gave a stiff nod. She disappeared back inside the house. Xavier's attention stayed locked on Claire. Hatred oozed off him. Moments later, Maribelle returned. She'd grabbed a shawl for her shoulders and held a postcard in her hand.

Claire stepped forward to take it. She angled the card

for Gavin to see. It was dated eighteen months ago and the zip code was from the Houston area. The lettering scrawled across the front appeared feminine. But there was no way to know if it was Stephanie's without having it examined by an expert. For that, Claire needed something else Stephanie had written.

"Do you still have some of Stephanie's things?" she asked. "A notebook from school, perhaps? Or a note she wrote?"

"No, ma'am."

Maribelle voice was flat. Rehearsed. Claire had the sinking sensation that she'd been coached by her husband. Everything about this encounter only deepened her uneasiness about Stephanie's whereabouts. She chewed the inside of her cheek. "Did Faye Hansen speak with you recently about Stephanie? It's my understanding she was concerned about your daughter."

Xavier's glowered. "We had nothing to do with that woman's murder. You're testing my patience, Sheriff. We aren't criminals, and I'm gettin' real sick and tired of being treated like one. All we want is to be left alone."

So he knew Faye was dead. Xavier might live in the woods, but he wasn't as out of touch as he liked to claim. Maribelle's expression stayed placid. They could've been discussing the weather for all the emotion she showed. But Claire sensed there was more going on under the surface. The older woman's hand trembled as she tightened the shawl around her shoulders.

Claire lifted the postcard. "I'd like to take this with

me, if that's all right. I'll return it when the investigation is complete."

"Don't bother." Xavier snorted. "We don't need it."

Claire ignored him, keeping her gaze on Maribelle. "I'll return it."

For a moment, there was a flicker of something in the woman's eyes. Gratitude? Worry? Before Claire could figure it out, Maribelle turned. She disappeared into the house. The screen door slapped closed behind her, like a gunshot.

"You've asked your questions." Xavier straightened. "Now go."

Claire turned. Gavin kept one pace behind her, using his body as a shield. Still, she felt the heat of Xavier's gaze following her into the trees. A shiver that had nothing to do with the cold weather raced down her spine.

FIVE

The conversation with the Whitlocks plagued Gavin as he drove to Wilson's Lakeside Cabin Rental. Xavier had a mean streak, that much was certain. Even his wife was afraid of him. Maribelle didn't answer a question or make a move without looking toward her husband. It was unnerving. But was he guilty of murdering Faye? It was too early to tell.

In front of him, in her own vehicle, Claire tapped her brakes and pulled into a parking spot. Gavin followed suit. She leapt from her vehicle, holding up a finger indicating he should wait, then went inside the main office. A woman was sitting behind the counter. They started talking.

Hold music spilled from Gavin's car speakers. He tapped his thumb against the steering wheel. Anxiety churned his stomach. He was waiting for his boss, Lieutenant Vikki Rodriguez, to come back on the line.

Faye's murder. Stephanie's disappearance. The

missing private investigator. Protecting Claire. There were a lot of pieces to this case and Gavin couldn't be everywhere at once.

"Gavin, sorry to keep you waiting." Lieutenant Rodriquez's voice was clipped but not unkind. "I've spoken to Ryker Montgomery. He's available to assist on the case immediately. As I understand it, you and Ryker have worked together before?"

"Yes, ma'am, as state troopers."

Ryker wasn't just a colleague and fellow ranger. He was one of Gavin's close friends. When an opening became available in Company A, it'd been Ryker who recommended Gavin for the position.

"Good," Lieutenant Rodriquez said. "I've also reached out to Grady West. He stands ready to assist as well, should you need it. Keep me informed, Gavin. Claire went above and beyond during the serial killer investigation. I consider her a friend and an honorary member of Company A."

"Understood. Thank you, ma'am."

He hung up just as Claire darted from the office. She got back into her vehicle. Within moments, Gavin was following her down a winding road lined with trees. They passed a log house labeled private residence. Her parent's home, maybe? A playground sat a short distance away. The road curved slightly and more of Lake Hudson came into view. The surface rippled with raindrops.

Claire stopped in front of Cabin 12. Gavin parked, grabbed his overnight bag, and raced to join her on the small front porch. "Please tell me you have heating. I've never been so cold in my life."

She laughed, brushing strands of wet hair from her cheek. "We do. There's a gas fireplace too."

The waning sunlight caressed the curve of her mouth and the delicate line of her jaw. Claire's gaze met his. Her eyes were the color of bluebonnets. Gavin's heart picked up speed, as any thoughts of being cold fled his mind. Suddenly, he was burning up inside his coat.

"Sorry, I have to..." Claire held up a key. A pretty blush colored her cheeks.

Belatedly, Gavin realized he was blocking the door. He stepped to the side. "Right. Sorry." He gave himself a mental shake. Yes, Claire was beautiful, but he needed to keep his focus on the case. And her safety. "How many guests do you have staying on the property?"

"Just five at the moment. Winter isn't a busy time for us, but there are a few fishermen who come year-round."

She opened the rustic wooden door to the cabin. Gavin crossed the threshold and whistled. The open floor plan was simple but decorated with comfort in mind. Wood beams lined the ceiling and picture windows over-looked the lake. Couches with comfortable pillows sat in front of a fireplace with a granite hearth. A full kitchen sat on his right. A hallway, leading to the bedrooms, curved to the left.

Gavin set his bag down. "This is beautiful."

"Thank you. My mom stocked the fridge for you with a few necessities, but if you need something specific, just let the front desk know. There's a coffee maker. Cups and dishes." Claire tilted her head. "Ummm, I can't think of anything else. I live in Cabin 11, which is just next door, so if you have questions, call."

"I'll be fine."

Claire hesitated. "I'm having dinner with my family. I'd love for you to join us."

The offer was kind, but Gavin couldn't consider accepting. He was attracted to Claire. There was no denying that. He'd known it the minute he saw her at Bennett's wedding in that stunning silk dress. But they were working together now and that complicated things. It required firm boundaries.

If he was being honest, even if they weren't working together, Gavin wouldn't ask Claire out. He'd steered clear of romance after his fiancée left him at the altar five years ago. He wasn't good at love.

"Thank you for the offer, Claire—"

A knock at the door cut off Gavin's reply. A large man stood on the front stoop, visible through the window next to the door. Light reflected off his bald head, and a thick beard covered the lower half of his face. Gavin recognized him instantly. It was Daniel Wilson, Claire's father.

She answered the door. Daniel gave his daughter a hug before stepping inside. He greeted Gavin with a friendly smile and a strong handshake. "Good to see you again, Gavin. I hope everything is okay with the cabin. I purposefully put you in the one next to Claire's. Figured you'd want to keep an eye out for any trouble."

He did. "It's perfect. Thank you, sir."

"I should be thanking you. My daughter can handle herself, but I'm glad she has you watching her back, all the same." Daniel swung his car keys around one finger. "Let me take you on a tour of the property before we head to my house for dinner."

"A tour would be great." Gavin had intended to take one on his own, anyway. Just in case. "But I'll come back here and eat something—"

"Nonsense." Daniel clapped him on the back. "Nothing beats my wife's home cooking. I insist."

There was no way to refuse without insulting the man. Gavin gave up the fight. He shrugged his coat back on and trudged out into the cold. The rain drifted into a light mist.

Claire zipped up her jacket. "I can't wait to see Jacob anymore. I'll meet y'all at the main house."

She gave a wave and jogged up the short walkway to the log cabin they'd driven past earlier. Welcoming lights shone from inside. Gavin waited until Claire disappeared into the house before turning back to Daniel. "I'm ready."

Daniel led Gavin to a beat-up pickup. "She ain't much to look at, but she runs like a dream."

Gavin got into the passenger seat. It was surprisingly comfortable. He sank into the soft fabric and rubbed his stiff hands together. He needed to find his gloves.

Daniel fired up the engine, and after adjusting the heat, took a turn leading them to the lake. "Claire filled me in on what happened today, but my daughter glosses over things so I don't worry. I want the truth. Exactly how much trouble is Claire in?"

"Hard to say, sir. There's no clear connection between Faye's murder and the threat against Claire, but it's awfully coincidental. I'd be surprised to find out they aren't connected."

"So would I. Claire and Faye were close as children. They'd drifted apart, as adults do when their lives go in different directions, but the affection between them was always there. Not to mention, my daughter has made waves since taking over as sheriff."

"It's my understanding Sheriff King managed the department differently."

"That's a polite way of putting it." Daniel arched his brows. "I'm a simple man, Gavin. I say things bluntly. Randy King was a terrible sheriff. He was constantly looking over his shoulder, afraid of losing power, so he insisted on working every case himself. He ignored evidence from time to time. He also made judgments about people."

"Like Stephanie?"

Daniel nodded. "Sheriff King labeled her a trouble-maker because of who her stepfather was. But he was wrong. I didn't know Stephanie well, but she attended the Bible study group at church. She was a hard worker. A sweet girl."

His assessment echoed Mary Ellen's. Gavin always dedicated one hundred percent of himself to each case, but hearing what a good person Stephanie was only fueled his determination to discover what happened to her.

"This town needs Claire," Daniel continued. "Fulton County is my home, but I'm not blind to its faults. We need an honest sheriff. One who does the job with integrity and fairness."

Gavin couldn't agree more. "I've already spoken to my supervisor. No expense will be spared on this case. We will get to the bottom of things."

"Thank you, Gavin. I have one more request. My wife is supportive of Claire's job, but she worries day and night about her. Don't bring the case up at dinner." He side-eyed Gavin. "I'm not saying Lindsey ain't strong. She's tough as nails, but her kids are a soft spot. Whatever precautions need to be taken, talk to me about them. I'll explain them to Lindsey."

"I understand." Gavin admired the tender way Daniel spoke about his wife. His concern for her well-being was evident. How would a love like that feel? Decades into a marriage with grown children?

He couldn't imagine it. Gavin had been alone so long, he'd given up any thought of growing old with someone. His career took all his energy. There wasn't room for dating or marriage. And maybe that was the crux of the issue with Claire. The spark between them, the one Gavin had no intention of doing anything about, made him notice the loneliness in his life.

He didn't like it.

"Mommy, mommy, mommy."

Claire crouched and opened her arms wide. Jacob's little body collided with hers, a bundle of curls and exuberant energy. She showered kisses on his face before lifting him from the floor into her arms. The troubles she'd walked through the door with melted from her shoulders. There was nothing better than being with Jacob. Her son was the center of her world.

He planted a kiss on her cheek and then wriggled to get down. "Grannie and I made cake. I want some, but she said I have to eat dinner first. Can we eat now?"

"Let your momma take off her shoes first, Jacob." Lindsey, Claire's mother, came around the corner from the kitchen. Age had added lines to her face, but nothing could diminish the beauty of her smile. She embraced Claire, hugging her tight. When she pulled away, concern lurked in her eyes. "I'm so glad you made it in time for dinner. How are you, honey?"

"I'm hanging in there." Claire gave her mother a reassuring smile. "It smells delicious in here. What are we having?"

"Roast chicken. Where's Gavin and your dad?"

"Dad's showing Gavin the property. They should be here shortly." Claire unlaced her boots and pulled them off. Then she removed her duty belt and placed it on top of the bookshelf, well out of Jacob's reach. "Give me a minute to wash my hands and I'll help set the table."

It was lovely to slip into family mode, to forget about the case for a while and talk to her mother about mundane things like the weather and Jacob's latest painting hanging on the fridge. The fragrant scent of chicken and mashed potatoes made her stomach growl. Claire hadn't eaten since breakfast over twelve hours ago. She stole a flaky biscuit from a platter on the table, broke off a piece, and tossed it into her mouth.

The back door opened. Gavin stepped over the threshold into the mudroom. Claire's heart skipped a beat at the sight of the ranger. A ridiculous reaction considering she'd only known him for a day, but there was something about Gavin that put her at ease...maybe it was the way he'd reacted when the sniper fired. Without thinking, without calculation, Gavin's first instinct had been to protect her. And yet, he didn't make Claire feel inadequate. It was a strange combination. A balance most men had trouble with.

Her ex-husband certainly had. Sam didn't work in law enforcement—he was an executive for a computer corporation—but his insecurity over Claire's rapid career advancement destroyed their brief marriage. He had an affair with a coworker. It didn't matter that Claire was pregnant or that they'd made vows. Sam declared he wasn't in love with her anymore. Their marriage was over.

One of the bleakest moments of Claire's life was being served with divorce papers while six months pregnant. Jacob had never met his father. Sam lived in Japan with his new wife. He wanted nothing to do with them.

"Everything okay?" Gavin asked, interrupting her chain of thoughts. He kept his voice low, probably so her parents, busy cutting the chicken at the counter, wouldn't overhear. "You have a troubled look on your face."

"Just thinking." She forced a smile. The last thing Claire wanted to do was talk about her failed marriage. "I'm okay."

The concern riding his handsome features didn't ease but, to Gavin's credit, he didn't push the issue. "By the way, my colleague, Ryker Montgomery, has confirmed he's coming. He should be here in a few hours. I hope it's okay, but I asked your dad if Ryker could stay in the cabin with me."

"Of course it's fine." Her father was probably relieved to have two Texas Rangers on the property. Claire was too. "I'm glad to have the extra help. This case is only twelve hours old, but it's getting more complicated by the minute."

"Agreed."

"Mommy, I'm hungry." Jacob's gaze shot to Gavin. His eyes widened. "Who are you? Are you a cowboy? You look like one. Except a cowboy should have a dog. Do you have a dog? Mommy won't let me get a dog until I'm older."

Gavin laughed. Claire smothered a smile and tried to look stern. "Jacob, that's not how you should introduce yourself. Offer your hand and tell him your name before you pepper him with questions."

Jacob extended one plump hand. "My name is Jacob Wilson."

Gavin bent at the waist so he was eye-level with the little boy. "Nice to meet you, Jacob. My name is Gavin

Sterling. To answer your questions, no, I'm not a cowboy. I'm a law enforcement officer. A Texas Ranger to be exact." He pointed to the badge on his chest. "I'm working with your mom. Dogs are great. I don't have one now, because I travel too much, but my favorite type is a yellow Labrador. Let me show you."

He pulled out his phone and tapped on the screen before turning it toward Jacob. The image of a Labrador puppy filled the screen. Jacob studied it. "I like those kinds of dogs too. What would you name him?"

Gavin's grin widened. "I haven't given it much thought. Any suggestions?"

Jacob tilted his head. "Lucky is a good name. That's what I would call your dog."

The two continued talking about a variety of subjects, from animals to building blocks. After dinner, Gavin helped Jacob with his Lego city. He was a natural with the little boy. It only reinforced Claire's initial impression of Gavin. Kind, steadfast, considerate. It also made her curious. Where had he learned how to interact with children? Bending over to look Jacob in the eye and speaking to him with smaller words wasn't natural for people who hadn't been around kids before.

Gavin mentioned over dinner that his dad died when he was two. He'd been raised by his mom. She remarried five years ago and lived in West Texas. Maybe Gavin had a lot of cousins?

The musing stuck with her as Claire and Gavin bid her parents good night before stepping into the freezing night air. Jacob was tired. Claire lifted the little boy into her arms and he nestled his head in the crook of her shoulder. His nose was cold against her neck.

In the distance, the lake shimmered in the moonlight. The boathouse was little more than a hulking shadow, but the walkway leading to Claire's house on the property was well lit. Gavin's gaze swept the area. Watching. Protecting. It didn't escape Claire's notice that he kept close by her side, in case of danger. It was comforting. Especially since carrying Jacob meant she couldn't reach for her gun.

The chances of the killer coming after her again...it didn't seem likely. Still, Claire was smart enough to accept Gavin's protection. Pride had no place when it came to keeping Jacob or her family safe. She kept pace beside Gavin. "I hope Jacob's questions didn't bug you. He can be something of a chatterbox."

"Not at all. I love kids." Gavin glanced at her. A blush tinged his cheeks. "I used to babysit to earn extra money. My mom worked two jobs just to keep a roof over our heads. Every little bit helped."

Another thing they had in common. Claire's family was doing okay now, but it took many years of hard work and determination to get their business off the ground. "We couldn't afford staff when I was younger. I used to clean the cabins for my parents during the summer. There's nothing wrong with helping your family. It teaches teamwork and responsibility."

They reached Claire's stoop. She set Jacob down and he started wriggling. "I have to use the potty, Mommy. Real bad."

Oh, no. He sometimes forgot to use the bathroom while playing until it became an emergency. Claire fumbled for the keys on her belt. "Give me one second to open the door."

"Hurry." He jumped from one foot to the other. His curly hair bounced with the force of his movements.

She undid the lock, and the door swung open. Jacob bolted past her to the bathroom. Claire automatically moved to turn off the security alarm. It took her a moment to realize something was wrong. She paused, ice flooding her veins.

The panel read Unarmed.

"What is it?" Gavin asked, pushing his way into the house. His hand was already on the holster of his weapon.

She didn't have a second to answer him. Claire spun. "Jacob!"

The sound of a gunshot blasted through the house.

SIX

Anger pulsed through Gavin's veins as he surveyed the handgun rigged in the bathroom. It'd been designed to shoot Claire, but had fired when Jacob opened the door. A bullet hole was buried in the wall about five feet from the ground. It'd sailed right over the little boy's head. He'd been scared but unharmed, thank God. Still, the echo of Claire's voice screaming Jacob's name, followed by the sound of the gunshot, would haunt Gavin's dreams for the rest of his life.

Texas Ranger Ryker Montgomery placed his hands on his hips. His button-down shirt was wrinkled from driving across several counties, as were his slacks, but there was no fatigue in his posture, despite the late hour. Ryker's expression was grim. "How did the intruder gain entry to the house?"

"He broke a window pane on the back door and flipped the latch. Claire has a home security system, but it's an older model. She set it when she left in the morning. It wasn't armed when we entered the house."

Ryker grunted. "Either the intruder knew the code or he had a device that disabled the alarm system."

"My guess is the latter. The only people with the security code are Claire and her parents. They change it every month."

Once again, the attack had been well-planned and coordinated. It was frustrating. No, it was infuriating. The killer was running circles around them. Gavin gestured to the handgun. "This could be the same weapon used to kill Faye. We need to compare the bullets."

"I'll put a rush on it. You think Xavier Whitlock is behind this?"

"It's possible. He wasn't happy about answering our questions, and I think his wife knows more than she's saying about her daughter's disappearance, but that doesn't make Xavier a killer." Gavin ground his teeth together, fighting back a fresh wave of fury. "One thing is certain, however. Someone wants Claire dead. And the killer isn't concerned about who may get hurt in the process. He fired on us at the bakery this morning and now this..."

Awful images played like a horror movie in Gavin's head. What if Claire had walked into the bathroom? What if the gun had been pointed lower when Jacob opened the door? It would've been a tragedy. Either of them could've been seriously hurt or killed.

He took a deep breath to calm his runaway thoughts,

but it didn't alleviate tension coiling his muscles. "We have to find this guy, Ryker. He isn't going to stop."

His friend nodded sharply. "You have my word. I'll do everything possible to solve this case. We'll keep them safe."

Some of the pressure bearing down on Gavin's shoulders lightened. He wasn't in this alone. As a general rule, Ryker didn't take life too seriously. Quick to laugh, slow to anger, his fun-loving nature made him easy to like. Ryker was also a notorious flirt, which helped in the dating department. But when it came to investigations, he left all humor at the door. Ryker would work day and night until the case was solved.

"Why don't you see how Claire is doing?" Ryker suggested. "I'm sure she could use a friend right now. I'll stay here and help with the crime scene technicians."

Gavin nodded. He was eager to check on Claire and Jacob. The last time he'd seen them, the little boy had been crying his eyes out. Both he and his mother had been terrified. With good reason.

Outside, the air was frigid and scented with pine. Red and blue turret lights on the various law enforcement vehicles strobed. Keith was standing on the walkway between the two houses, talking on the phone. He hung up as Gavin approached. "The mayor keeps calling, asking for updates. The man is driving me crazy, but it's better for him to bug me than Claire."

"Surely he wouldn't call Claire given what just happened."

Keith rolled his eyes. "You don't know Patrick Scott.

He'd call you at your mother's funeral if he needed something. Especially if he's going to be fielding questions from the media." The chief deputy rested his hands on his duty belt. "Claire's parents are being interviewed right now, but so far, nothing's come of it. We're working our way through a list of everyone who was on the property today. No one noticed anything suspicious."

That wasn't surprising. Claire's cabin was nestled in the woods. It would be simple for someone to slip in and out without being noticed. Gavin blew out a breath. "Let me know if you find out anything."

Keith nodded. "Will do."

Gavin continued to the main house and stepped through the front door. He removed his boots in the entryway to avoid dragging mud across the wooden dining room floor. From the kitchen, the murmur of voices filtered out. It was Claire's parents, along with the deputy interviewing them.

A fire flickered in the hearth. Claire was on the couch, holding Jacob. The little boy's head rested on his mother's shoulder. He was sleeping, his eyelashes casting long shadows on his cheeks. She gently rubbed his back. They looked peaceful together. The sight halted Gavin in his tracks. There were things to say, but now wasn't the time. He started backing out of the room.

"Don't go." Claire's voice was barely a whisper.

He hesitated. Then, on stocking feet, Gavin crossed the carpeted living room. He sat on the coffee table in front of Claire. Her gaze lifted to meet his. The haunted look buried in her eyes reached inside Gavin's chest and squeezed his heart so tight, it physically hurt.

Claire's chin trembled. "Jacob fell asleep half an hour ago. I should put him in the bed, but I can't manage to..." Tears filled her beautiful eyes. "I can't find the strength to do it."

Gavin's throat tightened. "You can hold Jacob all night if you want."

She clasped his hand. Despite the blazing fire, her fingers were cold. Gavin wrapped them in the cocoon of his palm, hoping to warm them. Tears continued down her cheeks. A war battled within Gavin. A part of him wanted to spring from the seat and hunt down the man who'd attempted to hurt her. The other part of him wanted to gather Claire in his arms and comfort her until she felt strong again.

She swiped at her tears. "I'm a mess."

"You're a mother who went through a terrifying incident. You're allowed to be a mess." Gavin gently touched Jacob's back. "Is he okay?"

"Physically, he's fine. Emotionally and mentally, too, I think. The sound of the gunshot scared him, but he only cried for a few minutes. Jacob's so young, I don't think he realized what happened. Or what could've happened." She sucked in a breath and let it out slowly. "Jacob and I will stay together in the guest room. My legs are so shaky, I don't trust them to hold me up while carrying him to bed. Do you mind taking him?"

A tenderness Gavin wasn't expecting swept over him. "Of course."

He gently lifted the small boy into his arms. Jacob's weight was slight, but significant. A beautiful blessing. His own child—lost when his ex-fiancée, Willow, suffered a miscarriage—would've been a few years older than Jacob.

The pregnancy hadn't been planned. Far from it. In fact, their relationship had been strained. They hadn't been a good match from the start, and it was embarrassing to admit, but Gavin had drifted away from his Christian values. When Willow became pregnant, he was determined to do the right thing and make it work between them. They got engaged.

Then the miscarriage happened. Willow left him a few weeks before the wedding. She didn't love him, never had, and losing the baby gave her a way out. The chain of events forced Gavin to re-examine his life. He started attending church again and renewed his relationship with God. It brought him peace and his career gave him purpose.

Love and children weren't things he thought about. But there were times like now, while holding this precious child, that Gavin ached for something more.

He shoved that thought out of his mind. It was a dangerous path to take. Jacob and Claire needed his protection. Nothing else. And Gavin owed them his very best. He couldn't keep them safe if his head was muddled with romantic notions.

"In here," Claire whispered, leading Gavin into a bedroom. A night-light glowed softly in the corner. She pulled back the covers on the double bed.

Gavin gently laid Jacob down. Claire pulled the covers over his small form and ran a hand over his hair before kissing his forehead. The gentle nature of her movements touched Gavin. It was obvious how much Claire loved her son.

She joined him in the hallway, wrapping her arms around her midsection. "I should go back to my house, view the crime scene."

It was a testament to Claire's fortitude that she was even thinking about it. Gavin wouldn't blame her if she never wanted to step foot in her cabin again. "That's not necessary. Ryker and the crime scene technicians are searching for evidence. Keith is interviewing potential witnesses. They've got it under control."

Her mouth twitched. "It's not often someone tells me I'm unnecessary."

"You've trained your team well. Especially Keith. It's a compliment to your leadership that they can do the job without you."

"It won't stop someone from trying to murder me." Claire leaned against the doorjamb. Her lips flattened. "I took this job thinking it would be a quieter change of pace. Instead, I'm being hunted by a killer."

Gavin kept his voice to a whisper to avoid waking Jacob. "I can arrange a safe house for you and your family. No one will think any less of you for sitting this case out."

"I can't. I took an oath when I became sheriff, Gavin."

"Your life is being threatened."

"Exactly. What do you think will happen if I leave

now? It'll send a message to every other criminal in this county that if you want to terrify or intimidate me, then you threaten my family. I can't do my job like that." Her jaw hardened. "No. I'm going to see this through."

"Then we'll make a plan to keep you safe." Gavin's gaze went to the little boy in the bed. "Both of you."

Claire woke with a jerk. Her heart raced and her pajamas were damp with sweat. Instinctively, she reached for Jacob, touching his sleeping form lying next to her. He was breathing deeply. One arm hugged his stuffed dog, Mr. Woof, and a pajama-clad foot peeked out from underneath the covers.

A tear dropped onto Claire's cheek. The nightmare— the images of Jacob hurt and bleeding—had felt so real.

Thank you, God, for protecting Jacob yesterday. Please continue to watch over him, over both of us. Guide me to make the right decisions. I need your wisdom now more than ever.

The prayer eased the raw edges of her emotions. Early-morning sunlight drifted through the pale curtains covering the window. Claire carefully slipped from the bed. She checked her phone. There was a loving message from her sister that brought a smile to her lips. Bea was still in Denver, completing a wilderness training. She'd offered to come home, but Claire insisted she stay several states away. It was safer.

They'd spent a long time talking on the phone after everyone else had gone to bed. There was no one who could comfort Claire better than her younger sister. Just seeing the sweet text message of support was enough to put some steel back into her spine.

There was a criminal to find.

Fifteen minutes later, she was showered and dressed. Her parents' bedroom was empty. The bed, covered in a handmade quilt, was neatly made. Belatedly, Claire remembered they were helping an injured friend with his ranch animals. Her mom and dad had likely been up since before daybreak.

The scent of fresh coffee drew her to the kitchen. Gavin was seated at the kitchen table, reading on his tablet, a mug resting at his elbow. The deep cleft in his chin accented the curve of his freshly shaven jaw. His long legs were stretched out in front of him, feet clad in white socks with red stitching. He'd spent the night on the couch as an added layer of security for her family.

Claire paused in the doorway. A mix of emotions clashed inside her. She'd avoided getting close to any man since her divorce, afraid to let someone past the protective barrier surrounding her emotions. But last night... Gavin handled the crisis and her tears with gentleness and respect. There was no denying the handsome Texas Ranger made her feel safe. It blurred the lines between them, and she didn't know what to do with that. "Morning."

He greeted her with a smile that warmed his chestnut-colored eyes and sent a flurry of butterflies flying through Claire's stomach. She barely heard his good morning back. Nerves made her movements jerky as she grabbed the carafe of coffee from the counter.

Claire took a breath, reminding herself to cool it. There was no need to be flustered. She and Gavin were friends. That's all they would ever be. She wasn't in the market for romance. The marks left from her ex-husband's abandonment and the subsequent divorce were carved on her heart.

All of her focus needed to be on catching the man trying to kill her. There wasn't room for anything else.

Forcing a normalcy she didn't quite feel, Claire poured herself a cup of coffee before topping off the one at Gavin's elbow. "Are you hungry? I could make an omelet?"

"Your mom made enough pancakes for an army. They're keeping warm in the oven. I haven't eaten yet. I was waiting for you."

Good. Breakfast was the perfect time to discuss the next steps. Claire had some ideas about how they should move forward in the case.

She grabbed two plates, along with silverware. A quick look in the fridge confirmed her mom had cut fresh fruit to go along with the pancakes. Sausage and eggs were also on a platter in the oven. Gavin hadn't been kidding. Her mom had made enough for an army. Claire arranged it all on the table. "We should call Ryker and tell him to come over for breakfast too."

"Let him sleep a while. We took turns keeping watch

over the house last night. Ryker's a grump first thing in the morning when he hasn't had enough rest." Gavin winked. "His bad attitude will give us both indigestion."

She laughed. "How long have you and Ryker been friends?"

"Years. I'm relieved Lieutenant Rodriquez assigned him to help with this case. Don't get me wrong, I love all the rangers in Company A. They're like brothers to me. But Ryker and I have worked closely together before. We understand each other."

"I miss that. The sense of camaraderie." Claire swirled a slice of pancake through a puddle of maple syrup. "I lost it when I became sheriff. There's a kinship with my deputies, but there's also a distance between us. I'm their boss. It changes the dynamic."

"That sounds...lonely."

She shrugged. "I can be. But I also enjoy being sheriff. I like having the control to make sure cases are worked thoroughly. If Stephanie's disappearance had been properly investigated, then Faye might be alive today. I wouldn't be in this trouble." She picked up her mug of coffee and took a long sip. "Have you heard anything about the private detective Faye hired?"

"I spoke to my colleague Weston this morning. Michael hasn't been seen or heard from since the night of Faye's murder. They've issued a search warrant for his cell phone, hoping to track his location that way. In the meantime, every law enforcement officer in the state is searching for him and his car."

"I'm worried about him."

"I am too."

Claire set her mug down. "It's clear I'm the killer's target. The best way to protect Jacob and my parents is to stay away from them as much as possible. I'll sleep in my cabin starting tonight and he can stay here with my parents for the time being."

She was dreading the separation from Jacob, but her feelings didn't matter. Her son had almost become collateral damage. Claire couldn't allow that to happen again.

Gavin wiped his mouth. "I've received permission from Lieutenant Rodriquez to have a trooper stationed outside the house 24 hours for their protection. It'll start this morning. Additional troopers will do extra patrols in the county. Coupled with your own deputies, it should prevent any attacks on your family."

She tried not to focus on the word should in his sentence. Nothing was guaranteed. All Claire could do was her best and then give the rest to the Lord. He certainly hadn't left her alone in this. Gavin was here.

Without thinking, Claire reached out and placed a hand over Gavin's. His skin was warm under her palm. "Thank you, Gavin. For everything. I'm glad you're here."

He lifted his gaze to meet hers. Something akin to electricity arced between them. The touch she'd meant to be friendly somehow morphed into something else altogether. Gavin's thumb traced along the ridge of her knuckle. Heat coursed up her arm.

She couldn't move. It struck Claire that this attraction she was fighting...Gavin was feeling it too. Suddenly, it all felt very dangerous. Like wading into quicksand.

She wasn't ready for this. Especially not now, with everything else going on.

Gavin seemed to sense her conflicted thoughts. He released her hand, and she pulled it away. Embarrassment heated her cheeks. Claire wasn't interested in a relationship and it wasn't right to make Gavin think she was. The threats on her life were wreaking havoc with her emotions.

She licked her lips. Her throat felt impossibly dry. "I'm sorry, Gavin. I shouldn't have grabbed your hand. That was inappropriate. It won't happen again."

"Claire—"

A knock at the back door cut Gavin off. Relief washed over Claire. She didn't want to have a complicated conversation about navigating their relationship. As far as she was concerned, they were friends. Professionals. That's how she wanted to keep it.

Gavin rose, his hand on the holster of his gun. "Are you expecting someone?"

"No." Claire rolled her eyes. "But killers don't usually knock. Stand down, Gavin. Let me see who it is."

She peeked into the mudroom. The top of the back door was glass, giving her a view of the stoop. A man wearing grease-stained coveralls shifted in place. It took Claire a moment to remember his name. Her dad had hired him as a repairman for the property last week.

"It's safe, Gavin. It's one of our employees." Claire

LYNN SHANNON

walked to the back door and opened it. "Travis, hi. How are you this morning? Please come in out of the cold."

"No, thank you, ma'am." Travis removed his ball cap. A shock of red hair created a sharp contrast with his pale skin. "Actually, you should come outside with me. There's something you need to see."

SEVEN

Gavin surveyed the destruction inside the boathouse. Storage cabinets, doors hanging precariously on damaged hinges, leaked fishing lures. Broken fishing rods were tossed in a heap. Life jackets had been ripped apart with a knife, the insides left trailing across the concrete floor. Spray paint decorated everything, except for the boat floating in the water nearby.

Ryker arched his brows. "Someone was angry."

"With me," Claire said from her position on the opposite side of the cabinets. She had her arms wrapped around her midsection, but her expression was hard. She jutted her chin toward the wall in front of her. "Check out the message the intruder left."

Gavin stepped around a few destroyed items. The toe of his boot sent a fishing bobbin skittering across the concrete. He inhaled sharply as the words spray-painted across the wall came into view.

If you want to live, Sheriff, then quit. Leave town.

Ryker huffed out a breath. "Direct and to the point."

"Whoever did this took his time." Gavin bent to examine the twisted lock on the storage unit. The door had been pried open with force, probably with a crowbar. "And he's strong. How did he do this much destruction without being noticed by anyone? There were deputies paroling the property the entire night."

Claire sighed. "We own 70 acres, Gavin. It's impossible for them to be everywhere at once. I also think there were several hours between two and four when no one was paroling. There was a car crash on Hillside Road. Some teenagers got the bright idea to race on the empty streets. No one was killed, thank God, but the scene required several deputies."

Gavin nodded. Of course. Fulton County didn't have a large department, and with the icy roads, they were stretched thin to begin with.

Claire sounded weary. The troubles weighing on her shoulders were increasing by the minute. And Gavin had added to them. He mentally kicked himself again for that indiscretion in the kitchen. He shouldn't have brushed his thumb against her knuckle. What on earth had he been thinking?

He hadn't been. That was the problem. When Claire placed her hand in his...all reasonable thought had escaped him. Which sounded simply ridiculous. He wasn't some teenager with his first crush, but a grown man in his thirties with life experience. Claire wasn't the first woman he'd found attractive. Nor was she the first beautiful woman he'd ever worked with. But everything about her broke down the carefully constructed walls around his heart.

A strand of golden hair fluttered across Claire's forehead. Gavin resisted the urge to tuck it behind her ear. She made him want things. Love. A family. But he wasn't good at either. Willow's words replayed in his head like a broken record.

You always put your job first. You'd be a terrible husband and an even worse father.

Her accusations had cut to the bone, mostly because they were true. He put his career first. Being a Texas Ranger was a part of him. Since his failed engagement, Gavin hadn't considered pursuing anything romantic.

Until he met Claire.

Being around her was easy and natural. Like connecting with an old friend he'd known for decades. She was funny and smart. Dedicated to her job, her son, and her family. There was a lot to admire about her, but these wayward feelings needed to stop. Gavin wouldn't add to Claire's troubles. She obviously didn't want to pursue this constant humming attraction between them. It was for the better. Gavin had a job to do, a killer to catch. And that's where his attention—all of his attention —would go.

He assessed the fishing boat, tied to a pole by a rope. His boots tapped against the concrete as he circled the vessel. Gavin frowned. "The intruder breaks in, pries open the storage cabinets, and trashes the place. He even writes a message in spray paint. But doesn't touch the boat. Why?"

Claire shrugged. "Maybe he didn't have enough time. A patrol unit could've scared him off."

That was a possibility. Truth was, this entire case wasn't making a lot of sense. Faye's murder, the shooting at the bakery, and the rigged gun in Claire's house were well-planned. This...this looked like a random act of uncontrolled rage.

Ryker was still staring at the message scrawled on the wall. He consulted something on his phone, brows drawn down in concentration.

"What is it?" Gavin asked.

Ryker pointed to a curly swirl located under the word town. "See that? The upside-down question mark. It looks like a symbol used by the Chosen. It's part of the logo on their website."

He tilted the phone so Gavin could see the screen. Sure enough, his friend was right. The symbols appeared almost identical. A memory needled the back of his mind. "I was doing some research on the Chosen last night. They tattoo this symbol somewhere on their body, usually in a visible place, so members can identify each other.

"Xavier has one." She pointed to her neck right above her jacket collar. "It's here. You can't see it all the time, but I noticed it once while questioning him about cooking methamphetamine on his property last summer."

"I take it you didn't have enough evidence to arrest him?"

"Unfortunately not. His southern neighbor complained of a funny smell and there were rumors around town. I investigated, but Xavier refused to answer my questions or allow me onto the property. A judge wouldn't give me a search warrant without stronger evidence. The case petered out."

"That mirrors some of law enforcement's concern with the Chosen. Xavier could be behind this. He was quick to tell us he had nothing to do with Faye's murder, but I don't trust him further than I can throw him."

Claire's brow crinkled. "Isn't it strange for Xavier to trash my boathouse and then leave a calling card? I don't trust him any more than you do, Gavin, and I believe there's something criminal going on with the Chosen, but they haven't avoided law enforcement scrutiny by being brazen."

She had a point. Gavin tilted his head. "We need to be careful. So far, there's no evidence linking these crimes together. We could be dealing with two separate things. You made Xavier mad with your questions yesterday." He waved a hand at the destruction. "This could be his answer."

"Again, that would only draw attention to him. It'd be easier for me to believe someone purposefully put that symbol on the wall, hoping we would focus on Xavier. The same way Faye's killer tried to make the murder look like a robbery by stealing the bakery's money."

Ryker rocked back on his heels. "What we need is more evidence. I'm going to call the lab and get them to rush through what we have. I'll also get forensics down here. If we're fortunate, the intruder left a fingerprint or two."

Gavin wasn't holding his breath, but it was worth a shot. "We also have the postcard Stephanie supposedly sent her mother. A handwriting analysis could determine if it's legitimate. But we need something Stephanie wrote for comparison."

"I've been thinking about that," Claire said. "Mary Ellen may have something since Stephanie worked for them. I'll call her and ask."

Ryker tucked his phone back inside his jacket pocket. "It might be prudent to pay Xavier another visit. I'd like to know where he was last night. I can do that after the forensic techs finish here."

Gavin nodded and then turned to Claire. "I think we're still on the right track. Investigating Stephanie's disappearance will lead us to Faye's murderer. With that in mind, I want to visit Sheriff King. I've read through Stephanie's file a few times and have some questions for him."

She wrinkled her nose. "He may not tell you the truth. Especially if he messed up. Sheriff King is protective of his reputation. He won't be happy that we're making it look like he messed up another investigation."

Gavin had little patience with individuals who took the oath of a law enforcement officer and then broke it. Sheriff King's reputation wasn't his concern. "I don't care whether he's happy or not. He *did* screw up Stephanie's case. And the sooner we figure out what happened to her, the better."

Randy King lived on several acres and maintained a working ranch. Cattle dotted the fields on either side of the long driveway leading to a house with a wraparound porch and white clapboard shutters. Giant pecan trees shaded the barn. Claire zipped up her jacket after exiting her vehicle. The sun was shining, but it did little to take the edge off the cold.

She joined Gavin on the walkway. "Don't be surprised if Sheriff King knows everything about the case. He keeps his fingers on the town's pulse."

The front door to the house swung open and Sheriff King stepped on to the stoop. Deep wrinkles crisscrossed his forehead and trailed a path down his cheeks. He was dressed for the weather in a flannel jacket. The belt buckle holding up his pants was the size of a salad plate, and there was a holstered weapon at his hip. His hands trembled as he reached up to settle a cowboy hat on his head, a physical symptom of the Parkinson's diagnosis that'd forced his retirement.

"Morning, Sheriff King." Claire lifted her hand in a wave.

Randy's gaze narrowed. He didn't care for Claire but was too polite to be rude to her face. That didn't prevent him from talking behind her back though. She heard the rumors. And ignored them. There was no sense in making Randy an enemy. She was smart enough to know there were times she might need him. Like now.

Randy met them on the walkway. "Horrible thing about Faye's murder. I'm so sorry, Claire. I know you two were friends. And these attacks on you..." He clicked his tongue. "Awful. I'm glad to see you're okay."

"Thank you." She introduced Gavin, and the two men shook hands. Claire waited until the pleasantries were over before getting to the point of their visit. "Sheriff King, we believe Faye's murder is connected to a cold case. Stephanie Madden's disappearance."

"I heard a rumor in town about that." Sheriff King tilted his head to indicate they should follow him to the barn. "I didn't want to stick my nose where it don't belong—I'm retired after all—but I think you're barking up the wrong tree, Claire."

"Why is that?" Gavin asked.

Sheriff King picked up a grooming brush before heading toward a beautiful quarter horse waiting nearby. "Because Stephanie ran off. I'm sure of it."

"How can you be sure?"

He raised his bushy eyebrows. His gaze flickered to Claire before settling back on Gavin. "Despite what you may have heard about me, Ranger Sterling, I investigated cases correctly. Faye called my office and said Stephanie hadn't shown up for work at the bakery as scheduled. It's not uncommon for adults to skip work from time to time. Still, I took Faye's concerns seriously and sent two deputies to Stephanie's rental home. Her car wasn't in the driveway. The house was locked up tight and there was no sign of any trouble, so they left."

So far, everything sounded correct. Claire would've asked the neighbors if they'd seen Stephanie, and checked with the young woman's family and friends, but that was above and beyond the norm. She didn't believe Randy was a bad man, or malicious, just misguided.

"We aren't looking to blame anyone, Sheriff King." Claire kept her tone neutral. She didn't want to make him angry. There was some information only he could provide. "We simply want to catch Faye's murderer. What happened after you conducted the initial welfare check on Stephanie?"

"We waited forty-eight hours and then Faye officially filed a missing person's report. I obtained a search warrant for Stephanie's rental home. A suitcase was missing from the closet. Clothes and other personal items, like her purse and phone, were gone. There was no indication of forced entry. No blood or sign of a struggle." He shrugged. "Based on our search, we decided Stephanie had left town of her own freewill. That conclusion was supported when her mother received a postcard from her several weeks later."

Gavin leaned against the fence. "Other than her mother, did anyone else hear from Stephanie after her disappearance?"

"Not to my knowledge. But I also didn't ask." Randy used long strokes to brush the horse. "Like I said, it appeared Stephanie left town. I wasn't going to use valuable resources looking for a woman who didn't want to be found."

"According to the deputy who took the missing person's report, Stephanie had paid her monthly rent in full just days before she disappeared." Gavin removed a notepad from the pocket of his shirt. He flipped it open to a page. "She'd purchased a new patio set that was delivered after she left. There was fresh food in her fridge. New tennis shoes, still in a box, were next to the front door. She left her cell phone charger, expensive jewelry, and a favorite coat in the house. She was also owed a paycheck from the bakery. A sizable one."

Sheriff King's gaze narrowed. A red stain crept along the back of his neck and onto his cheeks. "Are you accusing me of something, son?"

"No. I'm asking if you took any of this information into consideration when determining Stephanie left town." Gavin straightened from the fence. He met Sheriff King's hard gaze without flinching. "I've searched for Stephanie. She hasn't renewed her driver's license, nor has her car registration been updated. Faye hired a private investigator to find her. Now she's dead. The private investigator is missing and someone is shooting at Claire. I don't have time for games, sir. I need answers, not spin."

Sheriff King swallowed hard. "What makes you think the person trying to kill Claire has anything to do with Faye's murder?"

"Because I won't stop until I catch Faye's killer." Claire tucked her hands into the pockets of her coat. "I'll chase down every lead. I know Faye was looking for Stephanie. That means I'm going to be looking for Stephanie."

"Someone doesn't want you to find her..." Sheriff King sagged against a nearby bench. He was quiet for a long moment. Claire didn't think it was possible, but the man seemed to age in front of them. He licked his lips. "I genuinely believed she left town. Faye was upset, yes, but Stephanie had a host of problems she was dealing with. She'd talked about starting over somewhere new with several people."

Claire stiffened. "What problems was Stephanie dealing with?"

Randy snorted. "You know who her stepdaddy is, right? I mean, we can start right there. Xavier doesn't cause trouble in the normal sense, but I don't trust him. I've long believed he's involved in something criminal. Could never prove it though."

She'd heard the same rumors. Maybe Stephanie threatened to turn him into the police? Claire passed a glance at Gavin before focusing back on the former sheriff. "What was Xavier's relationship with Stephanie like?"

"They didn't get along but kept things cordial for her mother's sake. I don't know any more than that. But I would be careful. Xavier is cold and I believe he's capable of murder, but he also knows the Chosen is watched by law enforcement. I don't think he'd purposefully do anything to draw attention to himself. Murdering Faye, shooting at you, Claire, and threatening your family...it's messy."

Claire considered Sheriff King's warning. She also wondered about Xavier's involvement. Was it possible the real killer had left the mark in the boathouse, hoping it would trick them into focusing on Stephanie's stepfather? It was something to consider. Leaving such a blatant calling card didn't fit with the Chosen's secretive nature. "Can you think of anyone else who might've wanted to harm Stephanie?"

Sheriff King pondered the question. "She had an on-again, off-again boyfriend. From what I understand, their relationship was tumultuous. His name is Alex Sheffield. Works down at the animal clinic and shelter."

Shock reverberated through Claire. She knew Alex well. So had Faye. She'd catered fundraising events for the shelter. The image of Faye sitting in her SUV with a flat tire flashed in Claire's mind. The killer had driven up, pulled over to the side of the road.

Faye had gotten out. She'd trusted the person.

Could it have been Alex?

EIGHT

Furry Friends Animal Clinic and Shelter was one block off Main Street near the center of town. Inside, it smelled like a mixture of antiseptic and wet dog. The reception-ist's desk was empty. Based on the hours posted on the plastic partition, the shelter was due to close in five minutes.

"Hello," Claire called out, leaning over the counter.

"Give me a second," a male voice called. "Be right there."

She turned to Gavin and mouthed Alex.

He nodded. A yipping sound came from an open corral in the corner. Gavin drifted closer. Several puppies played in the open cage, rolling over each other in a tumble of fur and tiny black noses. A sign announced they were available for adoption. They looked like Lab-mixes. A yellow one with a white spot on his head came running to the side, tripping over his own feet.

Gavin smiled at the puppy's enthusiasm. It was tempting to reach down and pet the little fellow. But it wouldn't be a good idea. He was here to interview a potential suspect, not adopt a stray dog.

Claire came up next to him. "They're cute." A smile played on her face and there was laughter in her voice. "Thinking about taking one, aren't you?"

"Actually, I was thinking about getting one for Jacob. We had such a great conversation about it the other night." He winked. "Every boy should have a dog."

Claire laughed and shook her head. "Don't you dare. I mean, we will get a dog at some point. I'm just not ready yet."

She lifted her gaze to Gavin's, and suddenly, he didn't think they were talking about a puppy. His heart skipped a beat. Unless he was mistaken, there was a yearning in her eyes. It ignited his own. What was it about this woman that sent his emotions into a tail-spin? Why couldn't he shake these feelings for her? Gavin prided himself on staying in control. Always. With Claire, it was a struggle to keep his thoughts locked on the case.

"Sorry about that." Alex Sheffield's voice entered the room seconds before he appeared. Different shades of animal hair clung to his polo shirt, etched with the company logo. Mid-twenties, he had an easy smile that bunched his cheeks. "What can I do for you, Sheriff? I hope you're here to adopt one of those puppies. They could use a good home like yours."

"Afraid not, Alex." She gestured in Gavin's direction.

"This is Texas Ranger Gavin Sterling. Your name came up in the course of an investigation. You're not in any trouble. We just have some questions."

He flicked the sign on the door so it read closed. "Ask away. I hope you don't mind if I keep working while we talk. I have some errands to run after closing up."

"Not at all."

"Thanks." Alex collected a puppy. He offered it to Gavin. "Do you mind? I can only carry two at a time. You'd save me a trip."

Gavin took the wiggling bundle. It was the yellow fur ball that'd raced across the corral to greet him. The white mark on the pup's forehead resembled a heart, and when Gavin cradled him against his chest, he licked his hand.

Trouble. That's what this puppy was.

Gavin cleared his throat. "Have you heard from your ex-girlfriend Stephanie Madden lately?"

Alex looked up from his position, wrangling one of the other puppies. A flash of worry flickered across his expression before his eyebrows drew down in confusion. "I haven't, but you're the second person to ask me that recently."

"Who else asked you?"

"Faye. She came in...I don't know...like a month ago. I told her I hadn't heard from Stephanie since she left town. Faye was anxious to speak to her, but I don't know why." His complexion paled. Alex's gaze shot to Claire before landing back on Gavin. "Is that the reason Faye was killed? Because she was looking for Stephanie?"

Gavin adjusted his hold on the puppy in his arms.

"We don't know yet. Did Faye ask you anything else when she came to speak to you?"

"No. Only that she was thinking of hiring a private investigator to search for Stephanie. Faye never believed she left town." Alex sank into a chair next to the corral. He appeared shell-shocked. "Sheriff King insisted Stephanie had moved to Houston. I mean...that's what happened, right?"

Gavin ignored his question. "What was your relationship with Stephanie like?"

"Complicated." Alex ran a hand over his face and then took a deep breath. He rose and gathered the remaining puppies in the corral, holding them like footballs. "We dated throughout most of our senior year but broke up after graduation. Then we spent quite a few years going back and forth. We loved each other, but we were young. I don't think either of us was ready for a long-term commitment."

Gavin followed Alex into the rear room. Nothing about the vet tech's demeanor indicated he was lying or nervous. In fact, he answered their questions straightforwardly. Either he was an excellent actor or he wasn't involved in the murder of Faye or the attacks against Claire. "So when Stephanie left town, were you surprised?"

"Not really." Alex shrugged. "She'd talked about starting over somewhere new. There were a lot of people in town that looked down on Stephanie."

"Why?"

Alex snorted, taking the puppy from Gavin. "Take your pick. Because she was poor. Her stepfather is strange. Her mother was an alcoholic. The sun shines on Tuesday." He shut the cage and double-checked to make sure it was latched. "This is a small town. People don't need a reason."

The puppy came to the door of the cage and gave Gavin a sorrowful look. He averted his gaze from those big brown eyes. He didn't have room in his life for a dog right now.

Claire stood in the doorway. "What was Stephanie's relationship with her stepfather like?"

"Rotten. Stephanie thought he was mentally and emotionally abusive to her mother. She wanted her mother to leave him. Maribelle refused. Stephanie didn't like to talk about it much, but you could ask Heather Scott. She and Stephanie were good friends in high school."

Gavin didn't recognize the name, but Claire stiffened. "Do you know if Heather has heard from Stephanie since she left town?"

"Nope."

They asked Alex additional questions, but he didn't know any more than what he'd already said. He also had an alibi for the night of Faye's murder. Alex's house was in the process of being painted and he spent the night with a friend.

Gavin held the door open for Claire as they left the shelter. His gaze swept the poorly lit parking lot. Quiet.

Still, his senses stayed on alert as they walked together to the vehicle. Twilight had turned to evening as they were talking to Alex. There were a lot of dark spots a criminal could hide in.

Once they were safely enclosed in the SUV, Gavin turned to Claire. "Explain to me who Heather Scott is."

Claire fired up the engine and flipped the heat to max. "She's married to the mayor's son, Ian. She also works in City Hall as the mayor's media spokesperson. My office has been communicating directly with her, providing updates on the development of this case. She knows we suspect Faye's murder is connected to Stephanie's disappearance."

"And she never said a word to you about being Stephanie's friend?"

"No, she didn't." Claire's expression hardened. "And I'd like to know why."

———

"I was friendly with Stephanie, but we weren't particularly close." Heather picked at a piece of invisible lint on her lilac sweater. The color accented her ash-blond hair and stunning gray eyes. "I'm sorry, Sheriff. It didn't occur to me you'd need to speak to me about her."

Claire studied the woman sitting across from her in the formal living room. Heather was polished and soft-spoken. Her nails were painted a pale rose, her makeup perfect. She was stunning on camera and even more beautiful in person. But she was also incredibly savvy. Heather knew how to answer a question and deflect. It's what made her an effective spokesperson for Mayor Scott.

"How did you know Stephanie?" Gavin asked. He was sitting on the couch next to Claire. The rough Texas Ranger was completely out of place on the silk couch, cowboy hat perched on his knee.

Heather flashed him a smile that bordered on flirty. "We went to school together. Stephanie tutored me in algebra. We lost touch when I went to Harvard, of course. After moving back home, I'd see her from time to time in the bakery. We'd chat, but never about anything significant."

"At this stage of the investigation, we're talking to everyone who was friends with Stephanie. Anything you can tell us would be helpful."

"Of course, I'm happy to help in any way I can. It's horrible to think Stephanie's disappearance has anything to do with Faye's murder. To be honest with you, I have my doubts about whether or not they're connected. I always assumed Stephanie had left town and was living someplace else under an assumed name."

Interesting theory. Claire leaned forward. "Why would you think that?"

"Because of her stepfather, of course." Heather picked up a crystal glass and drank some water. "Stephanie was quite close to her mother, but she had issues with her stepfather from the beginning."

"We've been told there were arguments between Stephanie and Xavier."

"Daily ones. Her stepfather demanded complete obedience and his rules were...strange. Only a certain amount of juice every morning. No television. Hand washing their clothes in the stream on the property. Xavier didn't want Stephanie to attend her own high school graduation. She was lucky to have finished school at all. And dating...that was completely out of the question." Heather set the glass back down. "Faye was kind enough to offer her rental home to Stephanie after she graduated high school. It only made things worse. Xavier didn't believe Stephanie should live on her own. He used to show up at her home, all hours of the night, and make threats against her."

For someone who claimed not to know Stephanie well, Heather certainly had a lot of information. "So you believe Stephanie left town and changed her name so her stepfather couldn't locate her?"

Heather nodded, smoothing back a strand of silky hair. "I'm sure you'll find her living in a different city. Although, Sheriff, I would caution you. It might be best if you don't look for Stephanie at all. If Xavier catches word about her whereabouts, it'll cause trouble for her."

Claire chewed on the inside of her lip. Had she been too quick to assume Stephanie had been harmed? She could be living somewhere under a new name. It was difficult, given social media, but not impossible.

They could be chasing the wrong motive for Faye's murder. Claire hoped they were, prayed they were, because it would mean Stephanie was alive. A deputy in Claire's department was tracking down extended family members, contacting them to see if anyone had heard from Stephanie since she left Fulton County. No one had. As every new lead dried up, Claire's fears about Stephanie's disappearance grew.

Gavin shifted on the couch. "What was Stephanie's relationship with Alex like?"

"I'm not sure. Like I said earlier, we weren't close, especially after I moved back home after college. Most of what I know about Stephanie's relationship with her family came from conversations we had during tutoring sessions." Heather laughed lightly. "I'll do anything to avoid algebra."

Some of the tension in Claire's stomach eased. She was stressed and grieving, desperate for answers about her friend's murder, and it was causing her to be suspicious of everyone. Heather's explanation about her relationship with Stephanie made sense.

Somewhere inside the house, a door opened, and a man shouted hello. Heather gracefully rose to her feet. "Excuse me a moment; that's Ian. He went on a business trip last week and couldn't make it home because of the storm."

She left the room with a swish of her skirt. Claire massaged her temple. She'd had a brewing headache for hours that was threatening to turn into a full-on migraine.

Gavin ran his fingers down the crease of his cowboy hat. "Xavier's name keeps coming up in this investigation.

Everyone we speak to seems to think Stephanie had good reason to be afraid of him."

"I know, but I keep thinking about Faye." She pitched her voice low so their conversation wouldn't carry. "She wouldn't have gotten out of her car for Xavier. Or met with him at the bakery alone."

"I agree. But what about Maribelle?"

Claire's mouth dropped open. "You think Maribelle may have killed Faye?"

"No, I don't think she pulled the trigger. But she and Xavier could be working together. Maribelle could've met with Faye at the bakery, learned what she knew, and then slashed the tire on her way out. Maribelle and Xavier follow Faye after she leaves the bakery. When their truck pulls up on the side of the road, Faye may have believed it was Maribelle driving. That's why she got out."

Claire had to admit the scenario was a good one. Before they could speak more about it, the sound of approaching footsteps reached her ears. She rose just as Heather came back into the room with her husband, Ian. They made a striking couple. Ian's features were straight out of a modeling magazine. Athletic and outgoing, he was well-liked. Claire had met him several times during charity events. The Scott family owned a chain of grocery stores, and Ian was the CFO. But, like his father, he had political ambitions.

"Sheriff." Ian stepped forward to shake Claire's hand. "Good to see you again, although I'm sorry about the circumstances. My father told me about Faye's murder. I can't imagine why anyone would want to hurt her. She was a wonderful person."

"Yes, she was." Claire introduced Gavin, and the two men shook hands.

Ian stepped back and placed an arm around his wife. Circles shadowed the area under his eyes. "You'll have to forgive me for not inviting you to dinner, but I've spent the last few days wrestling with contractors over building a new grocery store. I'm exhausted."

"Of course. We were finished speaking with Heather, anyway. Thank you for your time."

"I'll walk you out." Heather escorted them to the massive front door and opened it. "If you have any other questions, Sheriff, please let me know."

"I will." Claire tossed the other woman a smile as she crossed the threshold. Movement out of the corner of her eye caught her attention. She turned slightly and noticed Ian in the entryway, watching the exchange. The line of his mouth was flattened and a muscle in his jaw worked. His gaze was fixed on his wife.

Heather closed the door. Claire stood on the stoop for a moment. It was unusual to see Ian upset. Maybe the couple had an argument on the phone before he arrived home?

"Everything okay?" Gavin asked from the walkway. The porch lights picked up the concern creasing his brow. A five o'clock shadow darkened his jaw. As impossible as it seemed, the scruff made him even more handsome. Rougher. Masculine.

She was so tired. And her head was pounding. Claire

was tempted to walk straight toward Gavin and lay her forehead on his broad chest. Just for a moment, long enough to find the strength to drive home.

The turn of her thoughts rattled her. A romantic relationship was the last thing she needed at the moment. But asking for Gavin's help wasn't a bad idea. Claire held out her keys. "Would you mind driving? I have a headache."

"Not at all."

He took the keys from her hand. Their fingers brushed and warmth spread through Claire at the simple touch. She ignored it. Instead, she focused on how strange it was to be in the passenger seat of her patrol truck. Anything to distract her from the handsome Texas Ranger sitting next to her.

She tilted the seat back and closed her eyes. Gavin fired up the engine. The soothing motion of the car eased the pain in her temples. She gently massaged her forehead. "Have you had any updates from Ryker?"

"Yes. Xavier refused to speak to him. No surprise there. The boathouse was swept for forensic evidence, but all the fingerprints collected were from known individuals, like your dad. Ryker picked up the notebook Stephanie used for work from Mary Ellen. He took it and the postcard to the handwriting analyst. We should hear something soon."

Progress. It was slow, but every inch forward brought them closer to the truth. Claire continued to rub her forehead. "What about the private detective Faye hired?"

"Still missing. Every law enforcement officer in the state is looking for him..."

Claire peeled her eyes open. Gavin's hands were tight on the steering wheel and his gaze darted between the rearview mirror and the side-view one.

She sat up. "What is it?"

"Someone is following us."

NINE

Gavin's heart rate jumped as the vehicle tailing them sped up. The roar of the engine cut through the night air. He glanced behind him in the rearview mirror. Visibility was poor. There weren't any streetlights on the country road and the moon hid behind a wall of clouds. "Dark blue or black truck. No headlights."

Claire turned around to peer out the back window even as her hand fumbled for the radio to call dispatch. "How long has he been following us?"

"About a minute. He pulled out from a dirt road we passed." Gavin weighed his options. This street passed by Claire's property. He needed to deviate. A road with better lighting would be a good start. If he could get a view of the license plate, they could get an ID on the owner.

The rear window of their patrol truck shattered. Gavin instinctively grabbed Claire and pushed her down into the seat. "He's shooting at us."

Several more bullets slammed into their vehicle. Anger, piping hot, raced through Gavin's veins. His foot pressed down on the accelerator as he tried to put some distance between them and the shooter. Dangerous, given the wet road conditions and the chance of black ice, but he didn't have a choice. The madman behind them was determined to hurt Claire at any cost.

Icy wind whipped into the truck through the broken rear window. Gavin didn't hit the brakes as the road curved. His mind raced as he ran through various evasive maneuvers. He prayed no one was coming in the other direction on the road. The last thing they needed was an innocent civilian getting caught in the shootout. Claire rapidly spouted off their location and the situation to dispatch.

The truck behind them increased his speed. Gavin gripped the steering wheel. "Stay down!"

Another spray of bullets rocked their vehicle. Gavin swerved to make them a harder target to hit. The windshield shattered, spraying squares of glass in all directions. One sliced his cheek, another his hand. He barely felt the cuts. "Claire, you okay?"

"I'm not hit." She stayed low and pulled her weapon. "You?"

"No."

He gritted his teeth as Claire turned and returned fire. The truck behind them immediately backed off. It then took a sudden turn toward the lake. With horror, Gavin realized where the shooter was going.

Claire's family. Jacob. He'd taken the turn that would lead to her parents' house.

Gavin slammed on the brakes. The seat belt dug into his shoulder and smoke drifted from the tires as the scent of rubber filled the air. He maneuvered the damaged patrol truck into a three-point turn. Every precious second it took made his chest tighten. In the passenger seat, Claire was speaking frantically to her father, telling him to move to a secure location in the house.

She hung up. "The trooper assigned to guard my family is doing a perimeter check of the property." She radioed into dispatch, ordering them to contact the trooper.

Somewhere inside his head, Gavin was grateful for her quick thinking and level headedness. It allowed him to focus on driving while she coordinated the safety of everyone else. The frigid air flying in through the shattered windshield iced his hands. His fingers grew numb.

He turned onto the Wilsons' property and blew past the main office. The lights were out. Claire's dad had given his staff a few days off and arranged for the few renters they had to stay at a hotel. It was good foresight on his part.

Gavin took the fork toward Claire's childhood home. The lights in the pretty log cabin shone like a beacon in the dark. He increased his speed. A flash of chrome on a side street caught Gavin's attention.

The black truck.

Gunshots erupted. The steering wheel under Gavin's hands jerked as several bullets hit the tires. He struggled to regain control of the vehicle, but it was impossible. They went into a spin. Metal crunched and more glass shattered as the patrol truck slammed into a pine tree. The engine sputtered and then died.

Claire. Gavin sucked in a breath and turned his head. His airbag hadn't deployed, but hers had. He pushed it out of the way. "Claire."

She lifted her head and blinked at him. White powder covered her face and a scratch from the glass marred the bridge of her nose, but recognition flared in her beautiful eyes. "I'm okay, Gavin. What happened?"

The black truck pulled out from a small side road. The shooter had laid a trap, using Claire's family against them, and Gavin had stupidly fallen for it. He fumbled with his seat belt. Numb fingers slowed his movements. "Get down, Claire."

He spared a quick glance in her direction. She was slipping low in her seat, reaching for her weapon. Gavin's fingers finally found the button and his seat belt released. He pushed open his door with one foot while pulling his gun.

"Texas Ranger," he screamed, loud enough for the driver of the truck to hear. "Come out of your vehicle with your hands up."

On the other side of the car, Claire had also opened her door and, like Gavin, was using it as a shield. Her gun was trained on the truck. Gavin's heart thumped once. Twice. He thought for a second the driver was going to listen to his instructions.

Then the motor revved. Gavin fired his gun, but the

truck kept coming. He was on a collision course with them.

No. Not them. With Claire. The angle of the truck would put the brunt of the impact on her.

Gavin didn't have a second to shout a warning, but in his head, he was yelling Claire's name. He threw himself clear of the open door, just as the criminal's vehicle rammed into the patrol truck. Metal screeched. Asphalt bit into Gavin's skin as he rolled across the road. Pain ricocheted through his shoulder. His gun tumbled from his fingers.

He landed in the grass on the opposite side of the street. Gavin lifted his head and his heart stopped. His vision narrowed to the two vehicles mashed together on the other side of the road. Claire's side of the patrol truck was crumpled against the trees. If she hadn't moved in time, she'd been crushed. *God, no. Please, no.*

Gavin stumbled to his feet. His gun lay on the road in the opposite direction. The black truck reversed in preparation to slam into Claire's vehicle again.

One step. Two. He wouldn't make it to the weapon. There was no choice. Gavin screamed and raced for the side of the truck. He would stop the man with his bare hands if he had to. The driver turned. Gavin glimpsed a black ski mask.

The wail of sirens erupted through the night air. Relief rippled through Gavin. Backup was coming.

Still, he kept moving toward the truck. "Come out with your hands up."

The driver ignored his order. He spun his tires,

tearing up the grass on the side of the road, and took off. Gavin didn't watch him go. He spun toward Claire's vehicle. She was nowhere in sight. Desperation stole his breath as he raced toward the place he'd last seen her.

Please, God, please let her be okay.

Hours later, Claire closed the children's book she'd been reading to Jacob. Her little boy was fast asleep in the bed beside her. He looked like an angel. His long lashes cast shadows on his cheeks. Wrapped in his arms was Mr. Woof, the stuffed dog he'd had since he was a baby. After the incident with the black truck, Claire had to see and hold her son. The memory of a shooter barreling toward her parents and child brought fresh tears to her eyes.

She bit her lip hard to keep from falling apart. Crying could wake Jacob. She didn't want him to see her upset. Her little boy was completely unaware of how close he'd been to danger. After Claire warned her father, her parents hustled Jacob into the bathroom by saying it was a fun game. Even after everything calmed down and things were safe, Jacob had wanted to finish building his car tracks in the tub. Claire had helped him. It'd eased her worries to hear his laughter and see the bright smile on his face.

Now, in the quiet stillness, the terror came rushing to the surface. Every muscle in Claire's body ached. She'd dived out of the way before the truck rammed her vehicle. By some miracle, neither she nor Gavin had been seriously hurt. Her patrol truck was totaled though.

Thank you, Lord, for watching over us. For protecting my family and Jacob. I'm scared, but I know we are in Your hands. I'm trusting You.

It was tempting to curl up next to Jacob and sleep. She would've gladly stayed there the entire night. An iron will and a strong sense of duty forced her to slip from the bedroom to face reality.

The house was quiet. Her father stood next to the dining room window, a cup of coffee in his hand, staring at the deputies processing the scene on the road. A handgun was holstered at the small of his back. He heard her footsteps and turned. "Jacob sleeping?"

"Out like a light." She joined him at the window. Keith, her chief deputy, was speaking to Gavin and Ryker. None of the men looked happy. Claire sighed. The shooter must've gotten away. "Dad...maybe it's time you and Mom leave. Take a vacation with Jacob."

"Can you be certain whoever this is won't follow us? Try to use Jacob against you?"

"No. I can't." She couldn't be sure of anything.

"Then the best place for us is right here. Ryker will stay in the other guest bedroom. We'll have a trooper outside. I'm armed, and there's a home security system. Cameras will be installed outside tomorrow." He wrapped an arm around her shoulders and kissed the top of her head. "I'll keep Jacob and your mom safe, honey. Concentrate on doing your job."

She hugged him, breathing in the familiar scent of his laundry soap. "I love you, Dad."

"Love you too."

When she pulled away, Claire could've sworn there were tears in her father's eyes. Daniel cleared his throat. "Your mom's knitting in the bedroom. Go give her a kiss goodnight before you leave."

She went into the master bedroom, but her mother had fallen asleep. Claire blew her a kiss so as not to wake her and tiptoed out. She would call her in the morning.

Outside, the air smelled of pine and grass. It was freezing. Claire zipped up her jacket and tucked her hands into the pockets. Most of the deputies had left. Her patrol truck was also gone, although glass and broken tree branches still littered the road.

Gavin spotted her. His long strides ate up the distance between them. Each step made Claire's heart beat faster. Scratches from the glass had carved nicks in his face. One along his nose, another above his eyebrow. His sleeve was ripped and his pants muddy.

He'd risk his life for her. Again.

The echo of Gavin screaming her name replayed in her head. Panic had layered the timbre of his voice. She'd seen him racing toward the truck with nothing but his bare hands, determined to protect her. There was no going back from that. No way for Claire to ignore her growing feelings for the handsome lawman.

Gavin stopped in front of her. "We're done with the crime scene."

His words brought her attention back to the case. "What's the update?"

"The shooter got away. The black truck was stolen from an adjacent county. We found it abandoned an hour ago. It's being towed to the evidence shed for processing."

Nothing. They had nothing. The killer was running circles around them, putting Claire's family at risk, and it was infuriating. What would he do next? One thing was clear. He wouldn't stop coming for her. Not until she was dead.

Gavin glanced at the house behind her. "Is Jacob okay?"

"He's fine. I was worried he'd be upset, but my parents did a great job of protecting him, both physically and emotionally. Jacob had no idea he was in danger." The last words clogged in her throat as the tears she'd been holding at bay threatened to overwhelm her.

Gavin lifted his hand as if to comfort her and then stopped halfway. Indecision flared in his eyes. Claire stepped forward and wrapped her arms around his waist. His heartbeat thumped against her ear, soothing and solid. She melted into his embrace. Gavin's hand cradled the back of her head, his other arm gently supporting her waist. This time, when the tears came, she didn't bother to hold them back.

He murmured words of comfort. Gavin's touch was gentle, undemanding, and tender. Claire sucked in a deep breath to gather her emotions back under control. "Sorry. I've been holding it together for my family and..."

He wiped the tear tracks from her face with the pads

of his thumb. "No apologies, Claire. You've been through so much. I'm surprised you're on your feet. Anyone else would be curled up in a ball in the corner right now."

She laughed despite herself. "Don't tempt me."

He smiled. Claire wanted to drown in his eyes. The way he looked at her...it was intoxicating. Now wasn't the best time to have a conversation about what was brewing between them, but she didn't have the luxury of waiting. Not with a killer chasing her down.

She took another deep breath. "Gavin, I care about you. There's something between us and I've tried ignoring it, but that's not working."

"That makes two of us."

His thumb trailed along the edge of her jaw, sending sparks through her. She couldn't think with him touching her like that. Claire reached up to take his hands in hers. "My divorce changed me. My husband cheated on me, left me for another woman while I was pregnant with Jacob. He's never even met his son. We were having problems in our marriage for a while, but I took my vows seriously. I thought he did too. I was wrong."

This next part wouldn't be easy to say, but she needed Gavin to understand. Claire didn't want to lead him on. He deserved so much better than that. "I'm not sure I can fully hand over my heart to someone again. Until this moment, I've never even thought of trying."

Gavin was quiet for a long moment. "First, let me say that your ex-husband is a fool. To have left you and Jacob...he's missing out in a big way."

Oh, heavens, she was going to cry again. Claire bit

down on the inside of her lip to keep her emotions in check. She wanted to hear what Gavin had to say.

"You and I, Claire, we're more alike than you know." He pulled her into his arms. "I have my own bumps and bruises in the romance department. This isn't the best time for either of us to make decisions. So let's not. We're friends, and when this case is over, then we'll talk again."

"I like the sound of that." She sighed, a sense of peace settling over her. Being honest with Gavin about her feelings had lifted a weight from her shoulders. Claire wouldn't have to keep questioning herself around him. They cared about each other. It was enough for now.

Gavin's cell phone rang, breaking the moment. He released Claire to answer it. The cold air rushed in to replace his body heat, chilling her. She hugged herself. From Gavin's side of the conversation, she gathered he was speaking to his fellow ranger, Weston.

Gavin shot a glance at Claire. She froze. Ice flooded her veins, erasing any last remnants of their stolen moment together. She grabbed Gavin's arm. "What is it?"

He lowered the phone. "Weston located the private investigator Faye hired. He's dead."

TEN

The next morning, Gavin followed Claire into a conference room at the Fulton County Sheriff's Department. His entire body was sore from the encounter with the gunman. Questions about the case kept him tossing and turning the entire night. Hopefully, the meeting this morning would provide some answers.

Seated at the table were the rangers from Company A. Gavin's steps faltered as he registered everyone's presence, including his boss, Lieutenant Rodriguez. She rose from her chair to greet them both with a handshake. "Sorry to crash the meeting, Claire, but once my team heard about the latest attack, I couldn't keep them away if I tried."

"Bennett's the only one not here," Weston said, as he moved to hug Claire. She looked tiny next to the former professional football player. "But he has a good excuse since he's honeymooning in Hawaii."

Weston clapped Gavin on the back and the two men

LYNN SHANNON

did a half-hug, half-handshake. The move was repeated with Grady and Luke. Each of the men embraced Claire. She asked to see photos of their growing families. The next few minutes were spent catching up with each other's lives. Coffee and breakfast were brought it.

Gavin's fatigue lifted as he listened to Grady's funny stories about toddler mischief and Luke's woes about sleepless nights with a newborn baby. He hadn't realized how much he needed a break. The case and the threats against Claire were weighing on him.

He was terrified something would happen to her.

Gavin didn't know when it happened, but somehow this smart, beautiful woman had slipped past his defenses. Hearing how her ex-husband left her, pregnant and alone, had broken his heart. She was amazingly resilient. Claire didn't need anyone to take care of her, but she sparked every one of his protective and caring male instincts. Gavin wanted to be there for her.

Could he do it forever? He didn't know. His own failed relationship with Willow haunted him. The words she'd hurtled during their last conversation were buried in his heart.

You'd never make a good father or husband. Your work is everything to you. There's no room for anything else.

"Okay." Lieutenant Rodriquez clapped her hands, breaking through Gavin's thoughts and drawing the attention of everyone in the room. "I hate to ruin this good time we're having, but we have a case to solve. Let's get down to business."

Like a switch, everyone in the room turned serious.

Lieutenant Rodriquez turned to Gavin. "Let's start with a rundown of the case so we're all on the same page."

He ran through the chain of events, from Faye's murder to last night's shooting. Everyone listened carefully. Then Weston took over to discuss the private investigator's murder. "Michael Grayson, thirty-six, former military. Did two tours in Iraq before opening a private investigation business. According to phone records, he received a call from a burner phone on Monday night."

"The same night Faye was killed," Claire interjected. "What time was the call?"

Weston glanced down at his notes. "Nine thirty. We don't know what was said, but according to Michael's secretary, he was meeting with someone about a case. He drove to a park on the outskirts of Houston. Police officers located him last night."

"Why did it take so long?"

"His car was in a remote location, hidden behind some trees. Michael was shot three times point-blank. Ballistics matched the bullets from his body to the ones taken from Faye. Both victims were killed with the same gun. That weapon was then rigged in your bathroom, Claire."

Gavin blew out a breath as the impact of evidence hit him. "The killer meets with Faye, slashes her tire, then kills her on a remote road. He rifles through her wallet, looking for the name and number of the private detective she'd hired. Then he calls Michael, arranges a meeting for the same night, and kills him. The next day, the murderer rigs the gun in Claire's bathroom, hoping to kill her."

Weston nods. "That tracks with what we know so far. One more note. Michael wasn't a trusting person. He had a handgun under his jacket and a spare on his ankle. Both were holstered. His secretary said he never met with clients or others in remote locations, only public ones. Whoever called him was someone Michael didn't believe would hurt him."

"Same with Faye." Gavin sat back in his chair. "What do we know about the shooting from the bakery? And the truck from last night? How do they fit in?"

Ryker opened a folder and pulled out a lab report. "Ballistics confirm the same weapon was used in both attacks. An AR-15. The rifle is used for hunting and professional shooting competitions. Half of Fulton County probably owns one. We didn't collect any fingerprints from the stolen truck. It'd been wiped clean."

"The killer is going to a lot of trouble to stop us from looking for Stephanie Madden. The real question is why. Why kill two people in cold blood and then try to murder Claire?"

"There are two reasons I can think of." Lieutenant Rodriquez tucked a lock of mahogany hair behind her ear. "One, Stephanie is alive but knows something someone doesn't want us to find out. Or two—and I think this is the more likely—she's been murdered, and the killer doesn't want us to find her."

"I don't think Stephanie is alive," Claire said softly. "The Houston Police Department did a thorough search and couldn't find her. We've spoken to every member of her extended family. None of them have heard from her since she left town."

"Sadly, I agree with Claire." Ryker removed another report from his folder. "A handwriting analysis was done on the postcard Stephanie supposedly sent from Houston after leaving town. She didn't write it."

Gavin had suspected it, but actually hearing the words out loud was a gut punch. The entire table was quiet for a long moment. This criminal had killed two people already—three, if Stephanie was included—and was coming after Claire. The stakes couldn't be higher.

Lieutenant Rodriguez straightened her shoulders. "I think we need to operate with the assumption that Stephanie is dead. If we get evidence otherwise, we can reevaluate. Suspects?"

Ryker leaned forward, placing his elbows on the table. "Xavier Whitlock could be involved. A symbol used by the Chosen was scrawled under the threatening message written for Claire in the boathouse."

"Does he have a motive for wanting Stephanie out of the picture?"

"Maybe. There are rumors Xavier is involved in weapons and drug trafficking. Stephanie could've uncovered evidence of his crimes and threatened to turn him into the police. They didn't have a good relationship." Ryker's mouth flattened. "Xavier refused to speak to me yesterday. We don't have any hard evidence linking him to Stephanie's disappearance, the murders, or the attacks on Claire. But he owns an AR-

15. He had it in his hands when I arrived at the property."

Gavin drummed his fingers on the table. "Claire brought up something the other day, and I think it's relevant. Faye trusted her killer. She wouldn't have gotten out of the car for Xavier. His wife, Maribelle, maybe. But even that is questionable. And from what we know about the private investigator, I don't think Michael would have met with Xavier on his own in a remote location."

Weston nodded. "I have to agree with Gavin on this one. Michael had been looking into Stephanie's disappearance. He would've vetted both Maribelle and Xavier, would've known they were part of the Chosen. I could see him meeting Maribelle in a public location. But at night, in the park? I doubt it."

"What about Stephanie's boyfriend?" Luke's brows drew down. "You mentioned him earlier. Alex. He admitted they had an on-again, off-again relationship. Those are typically volatile and can turn ugly."

"Alex provided an alibi for the night of Faye's murder," Gavin said. "He spent the night with a friend because his apartment was being repainted. But we haven't verified the alibi yet."

"I'll take care of it. Send me his friend's name."

"Thanks, Luke."

Claire blew out a breath. "Faye's funeral service will take place in Fort Worth, since that's where most of her family is. But there's a memorial service today at the church. I'm going to pay my respects. It'll also give me an opportunity to speak to Mary Ellen again. She knew Stephanie well and may provide more insight into Stephanie's relationship with Alex. Or there may be someone else we're missing."

"I'll go with you." Gavin was sticking close to Claire because of the threats on her life, yes, but that wasn't his only reason for accompanying her. Attending the service for her childhood friend would be painful. He wanted to support her.

She shot him a grateful glance. "Thanks. That would be helpful."

"What happened to Stephanie's car?" Weston was flipping through Stephanie's case file. He frowned. "If we assume she's dead, the killer had to get rid of her body and her car. That's difficult to do."

"I've been thinking about that same thing." Claire rose from her chair. On the wall was a map of Fulton County. She stood in front of it. "I think we should get a canine cadaver unit to search the lake."

Gavin inhaled sharply. Cadaver dogs were specially trained to detect human remains. Some could even locate a body under water. "You think the killer hid Stephanie's body in the lake?"

"Her body and her car." She pointed to a section of the map. "This area of Lake Hudson has several boat ramps, but they aren't used anymore because the entire area is a protected wildlife refuge now. If I was the killer, I'd drive Stephanie's car into the lake using a ramp. Or I'd get a boat and pull it into the lake."

"It's worth a shot," Lieutenant Rodriguez said. "I'll

arrange for the cadaver canine unit to do a preliminary search—"

A knock on the conference room door interrupted her. Keith popped his head in. "I'm sorry to interrupt, Sheriff, but Mayor Scott is here. He insists on speaking to you immediately. And, a word of warning, he's mad."

Claire observed Mayor Scott pacing the length of her office through the glass wall. He wore a designer three-piece suit with a dark red tie. His hair, more gray than brown, was elegantly brushed away from his patrician face. A glower marred his handsome features. Claire had heard the rumors of Patrick Scott's temper, but she'd never been on the receiving end of it.

Until now.

She wasn't afraid of him. Patrick couldn't fire her, but he could make her life more difficult. Claire didn't believe in creating problems unnecessarily. She leaned closer to Keith, keeping her voice low to prevent any of the deputies working nearby from overhearing their conversation. "Any idea what he's so mad about?"

"He refused to tell me. Sorry, Sheriff. I explained you were in a meeting, but he insisted on speaking with you immediately."

The door to the conference room opened. Gavin and the rest of the rangers poured out. A female deputy at a nearby desk stopped what she was doing, her mouth gaping open. Claire couldn't blame her. Every member of

Company A was gorgeous. But Claire's eyes immediately went straight to Gavin. He stood out. His chiseled features and gorgeous eyes were striking, but it was what was inside that really grabbed hold of her. He was brave and kind. Warm. Caring. Genuine.

Gavin's gaze shot to hers. Even from across the room, his look felt like a touch. It was electrifying and heady. And scary. Claire hadn't so much as looked at another man romantically since her divorce. Was she ready to try again with someone new? Was Gavin? He'd mentioned having his own scars from former relationships.

He shook hands with his fellow rangers, clapping several on the back, and then headed in Claire's direction. Gavin jerked his chin toward the mayor. "What's going on?"

"We're not sure. But he's definitely worked up about something. His pacing is wearing out my carpeting."

"Mind if I join you? I'd like to hear what the mayor says about the case."

"That's fine with me." She straightened her shoulders. "Let's do this."

She marched into her office. "Good morning, Mayor. Sorry to keep you waiting, but I was in a very important meeting with the Texas Rangers about the investigation. This is Ranger Gavin Sterling. He's leading the investigation into Faye's murder."

Patrick spun to face her. He planted his hands on his hips, nostrils flaring, completely ignoring Gavin altogether. The glare Patrick shot her could melt the skin off bone. Claire couldn't imagine anything she'd done to make him so angry with her.

"Why are you questioning my family about Stephanie Madden?" Patrick practically spit the words.

Perplexed, Claire moved behind her desk but didn't sit. "Heather and Stephanie were friends in high school. I needed to ask your daughter-in-law if she had any insight that could aid our investigation."

"Without speaking to me about it first?" A furious blush rose from his neck into his cheeks. He popped open his briefcase and pulled out a newspaper. "The media are watching your every move, Sheriff. They're all over this case. A reporter noticed you were at my son's house."

He slapped the paper down on the desk. A photograph of Claire and Gavin arriving at the Scott mansion was front and center with the headline: Police Question Mayor's Son about Recent Murder.

Patrick jabbed the paper with a finger. "Do you have any idea of the damage you've caused? This article alludes Ian was involved in Faye's murder, that he may have even hired someone to kill her."

A wave of sympathy washed over Claire. She didn't control the newspapers or the reporters, but false allegations like these were the perfect fodder for gossip. Ian would be questioned by friends and neighbors. No wonder the mayor was so angry. He was incredibly protective of his family.

She took a deep breath. "I will personally issue a statement clarifying Ian is not a suspect. Nor is Heather.

They were simply providing information to aid my investigation."

Patrick's jaw worked. It was any wonder he didn't break a tooth, he was gritting his teeth so hard. Claire could feel he was struggling for control. Beside her, Gavin reached for the paper and slid it closer to him.

The mayor took a deep breath. "The next time you want to speak to someone in my family, you need to call my office. Are we clear?"

She stiffened. "No, sir, we're not. I understand why you're upset, but I won't be dictated to. If I need to question someone about a case, whether they're a family member of yours or not, I'm going to do it."

The stain on his cheeks spread. He jutted a finger at her. "You need to be careful, Claire. Don't make an enemy of me."

"It's not my intention to."

Patrick continued as if she hadn't spoken. "Sheriff King understood the power of this office and the way elections work. He knew—"

"Randy King is no longer sheriff." Claire pulled herself up to her full height. She met the mayor's heated glare straight on. "I am. No one in this county, including you, is going to tell me how to run an investigation."

"What investigation? So far, you have nothing. You're screwing this case up, Sheriff, and I'm warning you. It's going to cost you dearly."

Claire could feel her own temper rising. "Are you threatening me?"

"No, I'm telling you how things work."

Gavin jerked up his head from the paper. His expression was hard, his back stiff. "Is the information in this article correct? Did Faye volunteer for your reelection campaign?"

Patrick's gaze shot to Gavin. He squinted as if sizing him up. "What difference does it make if she did or not?"

"Because Stephanie also volunteered for your campaign. Did you know her? Did Ian?"

"Of course we knew her, but only in passing. Most of the town knew Stephanie and Faye. There's only one bakery, for heaven's sake." Patrick clicked his briefcase closed. He glowered. "Sheriff, issue that clarifying statement immediately. And watch yourself. It's not wise to make enemies of people you'll need later."

With those parting words, he stormed out of the office. Patrick slammed the door so hard behind him, the blinds on her window rocked wildly.

Claire collapsed in the chair. Uneasiness churned her stomach. "That was...a lot. What is going on?"

"I'm not sure." Gavin placed a hand reassuringly on her shoulder and squeezed. "But I suspect people in this town are hiding more secrets than either of us realized."

ELEVEN

The memorial service was in the church annex. Photographs of Faye—from her birth all the way to adulthood—were scattered around the room. People encircled them, their voices lifting and falling like music. Gavin's gaze swept the room, noting the crowd in attendance. Faye had been loved.

Claire halted in front of a photograph. Two teenage girls, one summery blond, the other a darker brunette, stood in a kitchen. Faye and Claire. Their arms were wrapped around each other. Bright smiles crinkled the corners of their eyes. On the island in front of them were a variety of cupcakes and cookies. Happiness and friendship radiated from the image. It made Gavin's heart ache.

"This was the day before we started high school." Claire's voice was hollow. "Can you believe Faye knew, even back then, that she wanted to own a bakery? She spent hours trying new recipes. I hate baking, but she roped me into her projects."

She grew quiet for a long moment. "I should've made more of an effort to stay in contact with Faye when I went to college. And then again when I moved home. My attention has been on work, raising Jacob...I didn't make room in my life for anything else."

Gavin slipped his hand into hers. She was hurting. There wasn't much he could say to ease her pain. The best way to help Claire with her grief was to walk beside her through it.

She interlinked their fingers together and leaned her head on his shoulder. Gavin ran his thumb over the ridge of her knuckle. "Tell me more about Faye."

"She had this bubbly, fun personality. She ate her hot dogs and french fries with mayonnaise. And she loved pranks. Not mean ones, but anything that would make someone laugh. One time she filled my locker with rubber snakes. I jumped a mile high. We laughed about that for months."

"She sounds like someone I would've liked."

Claire tilted her head to look up at him and gently squeezed his hand. "She would've liked you too."

The look in her eyes tempted him to lean forward and brush a kiss across her mouth. He resisted. They'd agreed to be friends, and he didn't want to jeopardize the relationship by pushing for more than either of them was ready for.

"Claire." Mary Ellen approached them. "Thank you for coming."

Gavin released Claire's hand so she could embrace Faye's sister. The two women shared a long hug and a few tears.

"Do you have any news about the case?" Mary Ellen swiped at a lingering tear with a tissue. Her gaze darted between Gavin and Claire. "Maybe it shouldn't be my focus, but all I can think about is getting Faye's killer off the streets so he can't hurt anyone else."

"That's on all our minds," Claire reassured her. "In fact, if you're up to it, we'd like to ask you some more questions. Is there someplace we can speak privately?"

"Yes. Come on." Mary Ellen led them out of the annex and down a short hallway to a children's nursery. Depictions of Bible stories in bright colors decorated the walls. Tables and chairs, sized for toddlers, were arranged in a T shape. She shut the door behind them. "How can I help?"

Gavin hooked his thumbs in his pockets. "We believe your suspicions are correct, and Faye was killed because of her investigation into Stephanie's disappearance. Since Stephanie worked for you, I'm hoping you can help us narrow down who might want to harm her."

Mary Ellen sat on a table. Her shoulders curved inward. "I don't know. Stephanie was a sweet girl. She had issues with her family, especially her stepfather, but I think it became better once she moved into her own place."

"What can you tell us about Stephanie's relationship with the Scott family?"

She blinked. "Well, Stephanie volunteered for the

mayor's reelection campaign. She was friendly with all of the Scott family. Heather, especially. They chatted regularly."

Interesting. When they'd spoken to Heather, she'd failed to mention Stephanie's volunteer work and had downplayed their friendship. An oversight? Or a purposeful lie? Gavin wasn't sure.

"What about Ian?" he asked.

"There was a flirtation between Stephanie and Ian, but nothing serious. Some joking and a bit of teasing. Ian was involved with Heather at the time and Stephanie was dating..." Mary Ellen's eyes widened. "Now that I think of it, Ian's flirting caused Stephanie a lot of issues with Alex. He was incredibly jealous. I remember one time he showed up at the bakery and accused Stephanie of cheating on him. Alex was furious. Screaming and creating a scene. Faye stepped in and I thought Alex would strike her."

Alex didn't have a violent criminal record, but some people were good at hiding their darker sides. "Were there any other incidents you can think of?"

"No. It was just the one time. I didn't even remember it until now, otherwise I would've told you about it during our first conversation." Mary Ellen chewed her lip. "Do you think Alex could be involved?"

"I don't know." Gavin intended to find out though. "Keep this conversation between us for now."

"Of course."

Gavin and Claire said goodbye to Mary Ellen and made their way to the parking lot. Dusk was falling. The clouds had dissipated, giving way to a gorgeous Texas sunset. Any other time, Gavin would've stopped to admire the view. Instead, his attention was fixed on their surroundings and any potential dangers. He kept close to Claire's side. "Any thoughts?"

"My head is spinning with them. I—"

Her phone beeped. She pulled it out of her pocket and glanced at the screen. "It's a text from Ian. He's requesting to speak to us about the case." She glanced at Gavin. "He has information for us and says it's urgent."

The Westcott Country Club sat on a small hill overlooking the lake. Gold accents gilded the main lobby. Claire's boots were soundless as she crossed the marble floor to the dining area. Gavin kept pace beside her. A maître d', wearing white gloves and a tux, escorted them to a private table in the rear of the restaurant.

Ian was seated, waiting for them, his gaze lost as he stared out the window next to him. Dark hallows shadowed the area under his eyes and two days of scruff covered his jaw. He twisted a glass of whiskey in his hands.

"Your guests, sir." The maître d' announced.

The words brought Ian out of his trance. He stood and greeted both Claire and Gavin with a handshake. Pleasantries were exchanged. Claire pulled out a chair across from Ian and sat. Anxiety churned her stomach, but she forced herself to relax her shoulders. Ian had requested this meeting, and it was best to let him lead it.

Ian picked up the glass of whiskey and took a sip. "First, allow me to apologize for my father's behavior. I heard about the incident in your office. The article in the newspaper wasn't your fault."

Where was he going with this? Claire hated being suspicious of Ian's motives. She liked him as a person, but the more this case developed, the more questions she had. "You don't need to apologize for your father. I understood why he was upset. He's merely looking out for you."

Ian snorted. "He's looking out for the Scott family name. I'm just a part of that. But you didn't come here to talk about the issues I have with my dad." He licked his lips and twirled the whiskey glass. "How certain are you that Faye's murder is connected to Stephanie's disappearance?"

Gavin stiffened. It was so slight, Claire wouldn't have noticed, except that he was sitting close enough to have their arms touching. She kept her voice neutral. "It's a lead we're pursuing. Why?"

"I worked with Stephanie during my father's reelection campaign. She was a ray of sunshine and good at her job. Sweet. I cared about her. And Faye." He lifted his gaze to meet hers. His eyes were bloodshot. "I would look closely at Alex Sheffield. He and Stephanie had a volatile relationship. She broke up with him, but he wouldn't accept it. He stalked her. Called at all hours. Watched who she was with."

"Did she tell you this?"

He nodded. "She feared him. It made me worried for her safety."

Claire had the impression Ian cared deeply for Stephanie. "When Stephanie disappeared, did you report any of this to Sheriff King?"

"No." His gaze drifted out the window again. "I was foolish. I thought...it doesn't matter what I thought. I'd hoped—still do actually—that Stephanie is doing well someplace far from here." Ian pushed away from the table. "I'd better go. Heather will be waiting for me. Thank you for meeting me here. Since the country club is exclusive, we won't have any pesky reporters popping out to take photographs of us."

Ian took a final swig of his whiskey, draining the glass. From the flush in his cheeks, Claire was certain this wasn't his first alcoholic beverage of the evening. She'd never seen Ian drink before. And the gauntness in his face was recent. He looked like a haunted man.

He smacked the glass down on the table. "It's my wedding anniversary next month. Heather wants to throw a big party to celebrate here at the country club."

"Congratulations." Claire forced a smile. "You and Heather were childhood sweethearts, right?"

He nodded, twisting his wedding ring around on his finger. "We were destined to get married. My dad kept pushing and pushing. Fighting him...it's like resisting a tsunami. Impossible."

There was a thread of anger in his voice. Claire sensed there was a hidden meaning to this pivot in the conversation, but she didn't know Ian well enough to make it out. Could there be more to his relationship with Stephanie than a harmless flirtation? Had they dated?

"What is going on here?" Heather strolled into the room, her high heels not slowing her long-legged stride in the least. She wore a crisp business suit, her hair styled in soft waves that framed her beautiful face. Diamonds earrings and a designer purse completed the ensemble.

She halted at the end of the table. Her cheeks were flushed, and she cast Gavin and Claire a look of derision. "Haven't you done enough damage? The mayor told you to call ahead of time before you question any of us."

Her tone was caustic. Claire's brows arched. A smart retort was on the tip of her tongue, but she swallowed it back down when Ian rose from his chair. He kissed his wife on the cheek. "Don't get all riled up, Heather. The sheriff was kind enough to stop by and apologize for the news story in the paper today."

Heather opened her mouth and then snapped it shut. "Oh."

Ian glanced at his watch. "We should be going. We're late for our meeting with the event planner. Sheriff, Ranger Sterling, thank you again for your kind words."

He quickly hustled his wife from the room. Gavin's stunned expression matched Claire's own feelings. Every encounter with the Scott family left her more confused than the last. Through the open doorway, she watched Ian and Heather greet another woman with forced smiles.

"Ian's hiding something," Gavin whispered. "From us. And I suspect, from his wife."

Claire sighed. Another headache was brewing in her temples. "I know. But is he hiding a relationship with Stephanie? Or murder?"

Gavin slipped through a set of trees on the Wilsons' property. Frigid air, scented with pine and dried leaves, filled his lungs. Moonlight trickled onto the lake. Everything was quiet. And yet, Gavin couldn't shake the eerie feeling of unease inside him.

A state trooper sat in front of Daniel and Lindsey's home. Gavin lifted a hand in a wave as he passed. The lights in the house were dark. Not surprising given the late hour. He kept to the walkway, following it to the boathouse. He checked to make sure the building was secure.

It was. The door was equipped with a new lock that required a code to open it. From his vantage point, Gavin could see the back of Claire's cabin. The lights in the living room were on. She sat on the couch, reading something on her laptop, a fluffy blanket across her lap. The fireplace was on and a mug sat on the coffee table.

What would it be like to stroll in through the door, have Claire rise from the couch, and brush a kiss across his mouth? Gavin's breath stalled at the thought. He hadn't realized until this moment how much he wanted that.

Lord, I know we've been speaking a lot about keeping Claire safe, but I need more help than that. These feelings

I have for her...are they real? Am I ready to fall in love again? I don't want to make a mistake with Claire or Jacob. I need Your guidance to find the right path.

Peace washed over him. It didn't solve the problems Gavin was facing, but it reassured him that an answer was coming. He would keep his heart open and trust that God would lead him.

Gavin's phone beeped. He checked the text message. His heart skipped a beat when he realized it was from Claire.

Can you talk? I found something of interest.

Gavin jogged up the path to Claire's house. He knocked on the back door and she appeared a moment later. Her hair was floating around her shoulders in golden waves, face clear of makeup, dressed in sweatpants and a T-shirt. She was so beautiful, it took his breath away.

Claire disarmed the alarm and opened the door. She waved him inside. "I didn't realize how late it was before I texted you. Did I wake you?"

"Nope. I was doing a final perimeter check. What's going on?"

She led him into the living room and sat on the sofa, pulling her computer back onto her lap. Claire patted the couch next to her. Gavin obliged her silent request. The scent of her perfume tickled his nose as she drew closer to show him the laptop screen.

"The county has a social media page for event announcements and news." Claire clicked on a page and scrolled down. "As you can see, citizens post photographs they've taken while attending these events. I searched back two years ago, around the time of the mayor's reelection campaign and Stephanie's disappearance, and found this."

She enlarged a photograph. It'd been taken at an outside event. People were holding drinks, in small groups, talking. Gavin spotted Ian standing with Stephanie. He had his hand on her shoulder, his head tipped toward hers as if he was whispering something in her ear. Or kissing her cheek. Either way, the pose appeared intimate. In the shadows, Heather and the mayor stood by, watching. Both had scowls on their faces.

Gavin's stomach clenched. "Are there any more like this?"

"No. But this picture supports my instincts." Her expression darkened. "I suspect there was more than a flirtation between Ian and Stephanie."

Gavin's mind whirled with the possibilities. "They were dating."

"Secretly. Or, at least, they thought so. Alex was incredibly jealous. If he found out Stephanie and Ian were having a relationship, it would've enraged him. Unfortunately, all we have at the moment is a theory. Have you heard from Luke? Was he able to verify Alex's alibi?"

"Not yet. He called Alex's friend half a dozen times today, but no one answered. Luke will knock on the guy's door first thing tomorrow morning." Gavin couldn't resist reaching out to take her hand. "We're getting closer, Claire."

"I know." She squeezed his hand. "Thank you for supporting me today at Faye's memorial service. I knew it would be hard, but I wasn't prepared for how much. Having you there made it easier."

Her words sent warmth flooding through him. He lifted his hand to brush a strand of hair away from her forehead. Her skin was silky under the pads of his fingers. "I'm here anytime you need me, Claire. All you have to do is ask."

"I'm not good at that. The asking part."

She leaned closer, her gaze dropping to his mouth. His heart took off like a rocket, even as he stilled. Kissing her was a bad idea. A terrible idea. They didn't know where things were going and getting closer might only end in heartbreak, but for the life of him, Gavin couldn't get one muscle to move away from her.

Claire's mouth brushed against his, featherlight and sweet. Molten heat spread through Gavin. He pulled her closer, and when their lips met again, his heart opened. It felt like he was tumbling into an abyss without a safety harness. He lost himself, letting the world fade into the background as the kiss deepened. Nothing had ever come close to this.

He pulled back, breathless. It took everything inside Gavin not to lean forward and kiss her again. He ran a thumb over her bottom lip as fear niggled its way through his runaway emotions. They needed to have a conversation.

"Claire, there's something I need—"

The sound of breaking glass reached Gavin's ears half a heartbeat before Claire's security alarm blared. Ice flooded his veins. In an instant, he was on his feet, weapon in hand.

TWELVE

Someone was breaking into her home.

Claire grabbed her gun from the side table. She normally kept it locked in a safe, high in her closet, to keep it far from Jacob's reach. But he was with her parents. Since the attacks on her life, Claire kept her gun close by.

Gavin was already racing for the back door, his own weapon in his hand, determination etched on his face. Claire started to follow and realized she had no shoes on. With a frustrated growl, she wrestled a pair of boots onto her feet, losing precious seconds in the process. She didn't want Gavin intercepting the killer by himself. It was too dangerous.

The cold air stung her lungs as she slipped out of the house into the night. Gavin was halfway across the yard. Another shadowy figure dressed in black and a ski mask ran toward the lake. Claire leapt off the porch to join the pursuit.

"Police," Gavin shouted. "Freeze."

The criminal whirled. Lights along the walkway glinted off the gun in his hand. Claire dropped to the ground half a heartbeat before a bullet whizzed past her head. It thudded into the porch pillar. She rolled, seeking cover behind a wood pile. The thorns from a rose bush pulled at her clothes and pricked her exposed skin. She barely felt the sting. The sound of her heartbeat filled her ears.

Gavin. Had he been hit? She peeked out from behind the wood pile. Relief washed over Claire at the sight of his familiar form, unharmed, behind a massive oak tree.

The shooter ran. He disappeared into the woods. Claire rose and reentered the pursuit. She was hot on Gavin's heels when the sound of an engine filled the night air. Water on the lake rippled as a boat flew across the surface. The killer was getting away.

No. She couldn't let that happen.

"The boathouse." Claire skidded to a stop and changed directions. Her breath came in rapid bursts. Gavin's boots pounded behind her. She punched the security code into the door and yanked it open.

Her father's boat bobbed in the water. Another code in the lock box next to the door produced the key. Seconds later, Claire removed the rope from the mooring post. She shoved the key into the ignition and turned it. The engine sputtered to life.

"Hold on," Claire ordered Gavin. He grabbed onto a railing with one hand. The other kept his weapon at the ready.

She pushed the throttle forward and the vessel jumped free of the boathouse. Spray hit Claire in the face, chilling her overheated skin, as she steered in the direction of the shooter. His boat skimmed across the empty lake. He had a head start, but not for long. Claire upped her speed, pushing her small vessel to the max. They had to overtake him.

Trees whipped past as she shot along the shoreline. The steering wheel under her palm rattled in an unfamiliar way. Claire's initial instinct was to ignore it, but something about the engine's growl was also wrong. An urge she couldn't explain overtook her. She had to look at the mechanism.

"Gavin, take the helm." Claire screamed the words to be heard over the wind.

Without question, Gavin moved to replace her, his strong hand gripping the steering wheel. His gaze was locked on the criminal in front of them. Claire hurried to the back of the boat. She popped open the lid on the engine compartment.

Her heart stopped. Then a roaring rush filled her ears, drowning out everything. Dynamite sticks were attached to the engine. An old-fashioned alarm clock counted down the seconds like something out of a movie.

Ten. Nine. Eight.

"Bomb." Claire yelled the word, but the wind snatched it away. She whirled and raced toward Gavin. "Bomb! Bomb! Bomb!"

His head snapped to her. She didn't stop running or mentally counting down the seconds. The boat's engine slowed, as Gavin decreased their speed, and the wind lessening.

Four.

Claire grabbed Gavin's hand. She yanked him to the side of the boat. The lake water was inky black and freezing, but they didn't have a choice. Gavin must've come to the same conclusion because he grabbed a long flotation device, twisting the string around his wrist.

Three.

She scrambled up the side of the vessel, still holding onto Gavin's hand.

Two.

Claire's adrenaline and survival instincts were guiding her. All that mattered was getting off the boat. "Jump!"

Claire pushed off with her legs, flying through the cold night air.

One.

The boat exploded. Heat seared her back as the force of the bomb tore her fingers from Gavin's. The icy water enveloped her, shocking her with its intensity. For a terrifying moment, Claire tumbled through the darkness, lost and confused. Then she registered light above her. She kicked toward it, the boots on her feet slowing her down. She shoved them off with her hands. Her lungs screamed for oxygen.

She broke the lake's surface and sucked in a breath. Her hair was plastered to her head. Through the strands, the fragments of her father's boat were visible. Several pieces were on fire. Claire spun in a circle, horror stealing her breath. Where was Gavin?

He was nowhere to be seen. She screamed his name, the word coming out weak. Claire's teeth chattered. Hypothermia was setting in. Tears threatened to overwhelm her, but she shoved them back down.

No. Gavin couldn't be dead.

Please, Lord, help me.

"Gavin!" she yelled with all her strength. No answer. Her gaze flickered across the wreckage.

There. The flotation device he'd grabbed as they ran to the boat's side. Claire used long strokes to reach it. Her childhood summers swimming in the lake had made her strong and capable in the water. The freezing temperatures, however, could kill them both. If Gavin wasn't already dead. He was underwater.

Her fingers fumbled with the string. She found Gavin's wrist and hauled him to the surface. Moonlight and the dwindling fires from the explosion revealed a bloody gash on his head. He must've been knocked out by a piece of debris. Claire placed her finger under his nose, but couldn't tell if he was breathing.

There wasn't time. She needed to get to shore. "Don't you dare die on me, Gavin Sterling. Do you hear me?"

Her fingers and toes were numb. Claire's teeth chattered so hard, it hurt. She ignored everything. Keeping her gaze locked on the tree line, she swam. Claire prayed with every stroke. For strength. For Gavin's life. For her own.

Blessedly, her feet hit bottom. Claire hauled Gavin

closer to shore, using the last dredges of her energy to pull him free of the water. Her fingers shook uncontrollably. Still, she tried to find a pulse on Gavin's neck. His skin was so pale.

Nothing.

No. No. No. She screamed the words in her head, even as she threw herself down on his chest, pressing her ear over his rib cage. Her fingers were too cold, too numb to check for his pulse. She had to listen for his heartbeat.

Claire held her breath.

Gavin rolled his shoulders as he buttoned his shirt in the hospital bathroom. Every muscle in his body ached, and despite the pain medication, his head throbbed. The gash near his hairline required thirteen stitches. A mild concussion and nearly drowning had earned him an overnight visit in the hospital. The doctor signed his release half an hour ago.

He opened the door leading to his room. Claire stood next to the window. She'd been examined for hypothermia and released. Their near death experience hadn't prevented her from staying by his side for the entire night. She'd slept in the recliner next to his bed. Every time he awoke, in pain or confused, she'd been right there, holding his hand.

She turned, a smile playing on her beautiful lips. "You look much better than you did thirty minutes ago."

"It's amazing what a shower and clean clothes can

do." He crossed the room and pulled her into his arms. Claire sank into his embrace with a sigh. Her head rested against his chest. Gavin brushed a kiss across the top of her head, tenderness sweeping over him. "How are you doing?"

"Better now." She tightened her arms around his waist. "Let's never do that again, okay?"

"Which part? The bomb on the boat, nearly drowning, or hypothermia?"

"All the above." She tilted her head to look him in the face. "You scared me, Gavin, and I don't frighten easily."

The look in her eyes...it was his undoing. He bent his head and kissed her gently. These feelings between them were uncontrollable. And growing with every moment together. Gavin couldn't, in good conscience, continue without being fully honest with Claire.

He pulled back. "We need to talk. I know it's not the best time, considering everything that's going on, but things between us..."

"Are getting more serious than either of us intended?" Claire nodded. "I know. I feel it too. I care about you, Gavin. Pulling you from the lake last night, not knowing if you were dead...my feelings for you are deeper than I realized."

"It's the same for me, but I don't want to mislead you. Ever."

Confusion flickered across her face. "Okay."

He took a bracing breath, ignoring the faint ache in his lungs. "Five years ago, I was a different person. My faith in God had faltered, and my lifestyle showed it. I met a woman named Willow through some mutual friends and we hit it off. Marriage and a family weren't on my mind. I was focused entirely on my job, on becoming a Texas Ranger."

Embarrassment heated his cheeks. Gavin released Claire and turned toward the window, crossing his arms over his chest. "Willow accidentally became pregnant. Our relationship was on the rocks at the time, but I pushed that aside and proposed. I wanted to do right by her. By the baby."

Claire was silent. Gavin didn't dare glance in her direction. He wasn't sure he wanted to know what she was thinking.

"A week before our wedding, Willow miscarried. She was devastated. So was I. It's hard to explain, but the baby was real to me. I'd been thinking about names. Imagining a little girl with my mother's dark eyes or a son with my curly hair."

He swallowed down the bite of pain that lingered, even after all this time. He felt rather than heard Claire draw closer. She wrapped an arm around his waist and leaned into him. "I'm sorry, Gavin. That must've been incredibly hard."

Her kind words caused a lump to form in his throat. He placed a hand over hers. "Willow called off our engagement. At first, I thought it was grief talking. But then...she said I would never make a good husband or father. That my work is all that matters to me. She wasn't wrong, Claire. Being a Texas Ranger has been my goal since I was young. It's my life."

"I understand that better than almost anyone. My job as sheriff is part of who I am, but I won't lie. It's a struggle to manage Jacob and my career." She circled to stand in front of him. Claire searched his face. "I can understand why you're hesitating, but are you saying you don't even want to try?"

"I don't know." He cupped her face. "You're amazing. So is Jacob. You both deserve the very best. I'm not sure that's me."

A knock came on the door, interrupting their conversation. Gavin swallowed a growl of frustration and released Claire. "Come in."

Ryker pushed open the door. Mud coated the bottom of his jeans and his boots. A streak was on his shirt as well. Scruff covered the lower half of his face and his hair was sticking up in jagged peaks, as if he'd been running his hands through it. Dark circles shadowed the area under his eyes. He looked like a man who'd been up all night, probably because he had.

In one hand, Ryker carried a tray of coffees. Relief flashed across his features. "Good to see you standing on two feet again, Gavin. You still look terrible though."

"Nice to see you too. You don't look so great yourself. And what is that smell? Did you roll in a dumpster?"

"Nope, it's lake water." He flashed a grin. "You owe me, by the way. Not only did I make sure the paramedics got to you in time last night, but I brought you a double espresso with extra foam this morning."

"Hey," Claire chimed in. "I'm the one who dragged him from the lake. You can't take all the credit, Ryker."

They all laughed. Gavin took the coffee Ryker extended and, ignoring the fish smell wafting off his friend, embraced him in a manly hug. Then he shoved him away. "Ugh, you smell like a sewer."

"Not all of us got a luxurious stay in a warm bed with pretty nurses attending to our every need. I was busy working." Ryker settled on the bed, careful to keep his muddy boots off the sheets. "There's not much left of the bomb or the boat. Based on Claire's description, the device was homemade. I believe the killer planted it on the boat during the break-in a few days ago. The destruction in the boathouse was designed to throw us off track."

Gavin had come to the same conclusion this morning, once the grogginess of his pain meds wore off. "I underestimated him again."

Ryker pinned him with a stare. "We all did. This isn't just on you. Since the Chosen's logo was scrawled on the message written on the boathouse wall, I went back to question Xavier. He's missing."

"What do you mean he's missing?"

"His wife hasn't seen him for three days. I questioned neighbors and some known members of the Chosen. No one has seen him."

Claire sank into the recliner. "So Xavier could be the one behind this?"

"Possibly. I've got more news. Luke finally got in touch with Alex's friend. The one he supposedly stayed with on the night of Faye's murder." Ryker lifted his brows. "The alibi doesn't pan out. According to the friend, Alex arrived after midnight and was gone early in the morning."

Gavin stiffened. "So he could've killed Faye, and then driven to Houston to murder the private investigator she hired. Then he could've stayed with his friend, but got up early to be at the emergency clinic in time to shoot at Claire the next morning."

"Yep. Luke's picking Alex up and bringing him to the sheriff's department for questioning." Ryker stood, a grin spreading across his face. "Either of you want to join us?"

THIRTEEN

Claire stood inside the observation room of the sheriff's department. On the computer screen in front of her, Alex paced the interview room. Every once in a while, he muttered something to himself. His name was etched across the front of the polo and the shelter logo was printed on the back.

"He refused to talk during the car ride over." Luke crossed his arms over his chest. The ranger badge pinned to his chest reflected the light from the computer screen. "Alex already knew we'd discovered his alibi was fake. The friend must've spilled the beans after our conversation yesterday. Alex insisted on speaking with you, Claire, when I arrived to question him."

"I'm not surprised. We know each other casually, and I'm sure Alex thinks I'll go easier on him because of it."

He was wrong. But Claire wasn't above taking advantage of the situation if it meant catching a killer. She glanced at Gavin. "It might be better if you stay here and observe. The more comfortable Alex feels, the easier it'll be to get to the truth."

Gavin frowned but then nodded. "Take him something to drink. Maybe a snack too. It'll support his assumption that you're sympathetic."

"Good idea."

Their gazes met. Emotions tumbled through Claire, tangled and impossible to separate. When she'd pulled Gavin from the water yesterday and couldn't find his pulse, it became undeniably clear that her feelings for the handsome ranger were far deeper than she'd wanted to admit. She was falling in love with him.

And now...their conversation in the hospital only complicated matters. Gavin wasn't sure he wanted a wife and family. His heart had been broken—that was something she understood and sympathized with—but Gavin's hesitation also ripped at the wound left by her ex-husband's abandonment. He hadn't wanted a family either.

Impossible relationships. Claire couldn't manage to steer clear of them. She had no doubts Gavin would make a wonderful husband and father. He was kind and caring, generous and protective. But Claire had made the mistake of trying to convince her ex-husband that their marriage was worth fighting for. She wouldn't do it again. Gavin had to want their relationship to work as badly as she did.

Until he made a final decision, it was prudent to keep her own feelings locked down. She didn't want to be left brokenhearted again.

Claire tore her gaze from Gavin's. She focused back on the computer screen. Alex was still pacing the interview room, his movements growing increasingly frantic. He was muttering something, but even after turning the volume up on the recording equipment, Claire couldn't distinguish the words.

She considered letting him stew a bit longer but decided against it. Time was of the essence. It was possible Alex was innocent, and she didn't want to waste precious investigation time if he had a reasonable explanation for lying about his alibi.

After a quick deviation to the break room for a soda and chips, Claire entered the interview room. Alex immediately halted his pacing. He swallowed hard, holding out his hands in a classic sign of surrender. "Sheriff, thank goodness you're here. There's a simple explanation for everything."

"I'm sure there is." Claire offered him a reassuring smile and set the snacks on the table. She pushed them toward the chair closest to him. "Here, these are for you. Let's sit down, Alex, and talk. Before we do, I need to go through some procedural things."

She quickly ran through his rights and had him sign a waiver. Everything by the book. Whatever Alex had to say, Claire wanted it cleanly on the record. She tucked the waiver into a folder and gave the snacks another push in his direction. "Do you like this soda? If not, there's also water and coffee in the break room."

"No. This is great." Alex's hand shook as he popped open the beverage. He took a long drink. "First, let me say, I'm sorry for lying about where I was on the night Faye was murdered. I know it looks bad. But I didn't have anything to do with her murder." He lifted his gaze to Claire's. "You have to believe me."

There was a thread of desperation in his voice. Under the table, his leg was jittering. Claire kept her expression nonjudgmental. "Why did you lie to us?"

"I panicked. You said Faye's murder was connected to Stephanie's disappearance." He racked a hand through his hair. "There were some rumors, right after Stephanie left town, that I'd possibly killed her. It's not true. But Faye suspected me. I could tell from the questions she asked when we spoke last."

"If you didn't hurt Stephanie, then what do you have to worry about?"

He scoffed. "You're kidding, right? Sheriff, you grew up here. You know this town. My grandmother Jane raised me, and she's an amazing person, but my parents have a bad reputation. Drugs, in and out of jail. I started down the same path as they did, but saw the error of my ways when my grandmother had a bout with cancer. I got my life together for her. It took me years to rebuild my good name. People are finally respecting me. Another turn in the rumor mill would destroy everything I've worked hard to build."

Claire remembered the minor arrests for drug possession on Alex's criminal record. The last one had been two years ago. It was in the same time frame that Stephanie disappeared. Could he have killed her while under the influence? Had Faye figured that out? It was possible.

She needed to be careful with her questions. Claire needed Alex to feel they were on the same side. It was the only way he'd continue talking. "Rumors can cause damage. I don't blame you for being worried, especially since you and Stephanie had several public arguments."

Alex's leg bounced faster. "I regret those. I was using at the time and...I wasn't always a nice guy to Stephanie. But I never hurt her."

"Faye said you got aggressive in the bakery. She was scared you'd hit her."

"I know. I came back days later and apologized for my behavior. She encouraged me to seek help." Alex blinked rapidly, as if holding back tears. "Faye was... special. One of the few people in town who treated me kindly even when I didn't deserve it."

Claire couldn't tell if his emotions were genuine. Alex had lied to them once. There was nothing to prevent him from doing it again. "What did you and Stephanie argue about?"

"That day, I was upset because I'd heard a rumor she was dating someone else. We'd had an on-again, off-again relationship for years. I loved her, but Stephanie made it clear she wouldn't stay with someone on drugs." He twisted the soda can in his hands. "She was right, of course, but I couldn't see it at the time."

"Who was she dating?"

"I don't know. Stephanie wouldn't tell me, but the relationship was serious. That's why I flipped out. She said we were done for good and she was moving on, happy." He bit his lip. "When she left town, I assumed it was with the guy she'd been seeing. Then Faye came around, asking questions...she believed Stephanie was dead. Then Faye was killed. It scared me. I didn't want to be a suspect."

But he was. Alex could've killed Stephanie in a jealous rage and then murdered Faye because she was getting close to the truth. Claire's stomach churned at the thought. It took every ounce of training to keep her expression neutral. "Where were you on the night Stephanie disappeared?"

"Home. Alone." Alex met her gaze again. "I promise you, Sheriff. I had nothing to do with Faye's murder or Stephanie's—"

A knock interrupted his statement. Claire nearly growled at the interruption. She pushed a pad of paper toward Alex. "Help me prove you had nothing to do with this. I want you to write everywhere you've been and everything you've done for the last three days."

Confusion flickered across his face. "Three days?"

"Yes." Whoever had killed Faye was also attempting to murder Claire. That was the one niggle working in the back of her mind. Alex might have a motive for killing Faye if he'd hurt Stephanie, but why get rid of Claire? He had no sway over who the next sheriff would be.

Then again, he could simply be hoping Claire's replacement would bungle the investigation by not bothering to look for Stephanie.

Another knock came on the door. Claire handed Alex a pen. "The last three days. Everything."

She turned and marched to the door, ready to give

whoever was on the other side a piece of her mind for interrupting the interview. Claire swung open the door and the angry words died on her lips. Gavin stood in the hall. His expression was grave, his dark eyes haunted.

This was bad.

"Is it Jacob?" Her heart battered against her rib cage.

"No. No, Claire. Jacob's fine." Gavin placed a hand on her arm, but the haunted look never left his eyes. "I've received a call from the divers searching the lake. They've found Stephanie's car. There's a body inside."

Gavin poured a cup of coffee, exhaustion seeping into his bones. The long days and sleepless nights were catching up to him. Nearly drowning less than twenty-four hours ago—had it only been last night?—exacerbated the situation. And today...today had been incredibly difficult. The body pulled from the passenger side of Stephanie's vehicle had been bound hand and foot. The case was classified as a homicide. Ryker attended the autopsy and was heading back to update Gavin and Claire.

The evening news filtered from the living room television. Claire's parents were nestled on the couch together. Gavin didn't want to intrude on their quiet moment. He leaned against the counter and sipped his coffee. Claire was getting Jacob ready for bed. She'd be down soon.

Moments later, the patter of feet proceeded Jacob into the kitchen. The little boy wore footed pajamas with a cartoon pattern. His hair, still damp from the bath, was combed away from his face. "Mr. Gavin, I have a surprise for you."

Claire appeared in the doorway. She'd shed her police uniform earlier in the evening, exchanging it for sweatpants and a long-sleeved shirt. Her hair flowed down her back in a golden wave. She offered Gavin a brilliant smile that made his toes curl. Her eyes twinkled with amusement. The thirty minutes she'd spent with Jacob had done her a world of good.

Gavin set his coffee mug on the counter and dropped to Jacob's level. "A surprise? For me?"

Jacob nodded. He whipped out a piece of paper from behind his back and thrust it in Gavin's direction. It was a drawing. Streaks of green and blue formed the earth and sky. Several crayon figures of different sizes stood on opposite ends of the paper.

Jacob's chubby finger pointed to a tall person with wild black hair. "That's you. And this is your dog, Lucky."

Gavin grinned. A large star was pinned to his chest in the drawing. Lucky, his imaginary pet, was a blob of yellow with a fluffy tail. "He looks like a very nice dog. Who are these people?" He pointed to the two figures on the opposite side of the page.

"That's mommy and me. We're coming to visit you and Lucky." Jacob paused, worry entering his gaze. "If you get a dog, you'll let me come play with him, won't you?"

"Of course. You can come to my house any time, as long as it's okay with your mom."

Jacob threw his arms around Gavin's neck. "Thank you, Mr. Gavin."

He embraced the little boy. Tenderness swept through Gavin, wriggling past the last brick of his defenses. He imagined the life in Jacob's drawing. A house, Claire and Jacob, and a dog named Lucky. Family. Love. It made his heart ache.

He lifted his gaze to Claire. Were those tears shimmering in her eyes? She'd sucked in her bottom lip and nibbled it. Worry shadowed the curves of her face. Gavin was skirting dangerous territory. He hadn't promised Jacob anything more than he could deliver, but children didn't see things the same way adults did.

Claire cleared her throat. "Come on, little man. It's time for bed."

Gavin released Jacob. He scampered across the room. Claire took his hand, and they left, the scent of baby shampoo lingering in their wake. Silence settled in the kitchen. Gavin stared at the crayon drawing in his hand. He ran a finger over the dog.

A part of him wanted to throw caution to the wind and dive into a potential future with Claire. But a whisper of doubt held him back. What if he wasn't capable of being a good husband? Or father? His fellow rangers balanced work and a family, but Gavin had already failed at it once. He didn't want to hurt Claire or Jacob. Ever.

The back door opened. Ryker stepped inside,

bringing a wave of cold air with him. He shrugged off his jacket and hung it on a peg by the door before toeing off his boots. Gavin poured him a cup of coffee and set it on the table. Then he pulled a plate of food from the oven. "Claire's mom set this aside for you. Hungry?"

"Starving." Ryker took a long sip of his coffee before pulling out a chair. He bowed his head and said a quick grace. He forked a piece of brisket, shoveled it in, and moaned. "Do you think Claire's mom will keep cooking like this for me after the case is over?"

Gavin laughed. "You can't move into their house permanently. They aren't looking to adopt a six-foot Texas Ranger."

"Shame."

The two men chatted while Ryker ate. There was no sense in talking about the case, since Claire would want to hear the update as well. She reentered the kitchen a few minutes later, this time without Jacob, and joined the men at the table. Her shoulders were stiff and the easy smile from earlier was gone.

Ryker pushed his empty plate away. He swiped at his mouth with a napkin. "Using dental records, the coroner officially ID'd our victim from the lake. It's Stephanie Madden."

Claire closed her eyes. "The facts didn't support it, but I kept hoping this would have a different ending."

"We all did." Gavin turned to his friend. "Cause of death?"

"Stephanie was shot several times. We found 9mm

casings in the vehicle and a Glock under the driver's seat of the vehicle."

An icy chill settled in Gavin's bones. Faye had also been shot multiple times with a handgun. So had the private detective she hired. "The similarity between Stephanie's murder and the others—Valerie and the private detective—is enough to indicate we're dealing with a single killer. He didn't use the same gun in all three crimes, but he used the same method."

"Agreed. I believe Claire's theory about the case was right the entire time. Someone didn't want us locating Stephanie's body. I'm hoping the gun can lead us to the killer. I've sent it to the lab for analysis." Ryker pulled out his phone and scrolled to a photograph of Stephanie's vehicle. He set it on the table. "See the rope tied to the front grill? The killer shot Stephanie and then used a boat to pull her car into the lake using this nearby ramp. That boat could be the same one that lured you guys into a chase the other night."

Claire sat back in her chair. "Then we should eliminate Alex from the suspect list. He doesn't own a boat. No one in his family does."

"He could've stolen it," Gavin suggested. "Or borrowed it."

"Both times?" Her nose wrinkled. "Possible, but risky. With Stephanie's murder, the killer had to drive the boat to the ramp and leave it there for at least an hour. The boat could've been reported missing."

She had a point. Still, Alex had a clear motive. "He

admitted he was jealous and believed Stephanie was dating someone else."

"I know. We can't remove him from the suspect list, but I have my doubts about him. Alex doesn't seem smart enough to have planned and executed a series of complicated murders. His alibi wasn't even well thought out." Claire frowned. "Xavier, however, is a different story. He has a boat, he's still missing, and he's smart. Law enforcement suspects him of other crimes, but he's evaded arrest so far. If Stephanie discovered something illegal her stepfather was doing and threatened to turn him over to the police...he's capable of killing her."

"He also knows about bombs," Ryker interjected. "Grady did some digging into Xavier's background and discovered he spent time in the military. Explosives expert. He could've built the bomb that was on your boat, Claire."

Gavin blew out a breath. "We need to speak to Stephanie's mom again. She knows more than she's saying."

Ryker shook his head. "She's refused to talk to us so far."

"Things are different now." A shadow crossed Claire's face. "Maribelle is hoping Stephanie is alive. That's not the case. Hearing about her daughter's murder may change her mind about helping us, especially since Xavier is missing. This may be the best chance we have of getting to the truth."

FOURTEEN

Morning sunshine filtered through the trees as Claire stepped onto Maribelle Sterling's front porch. The weathered wood creaked under her boots. She was dreading this conversation. A death notification was never easy, but Xavier's potential involvement in the murder made things even more complicated.

Gavin stepped onto the porch beside Claire. His broad shoulders were encased in a heavy jacket, his holstered weapon visible underneath. Strength and competence oozed from him. The hardened man next to her was a far cry from the one who'd tenderly hugged her son yesterday. Both made her heart skip a beat.

She shook off her wayward thoughts. There was a possibility Gavin would close this case, leave town, and never look back. She would be wise to guard her heart. Along with her son's. They hadn't been enough for her ex-husband. There no need to risk being hurt like that again.

Claire formed a fist and knocked on the front door. Shuffling came from inside moments before the curtain on a nearby window shifted. Half of Maribelle's face was visible. A watery blue eye widened at the sight of them on her porch, but she didn't move to open the door.

"I need to speak to you, Mrs. Whitlock." Claire held up the postcard she'd taken from Stephanie's mother during their last conversation. "It's about your daughter. It's important."

The curtain fluttered again as Maribelle disappeared from sight. Seconds later, the lock snicked and the front door opened. Claire cast a quick glance at Gavin before focusing on the older woman in front of them. Maribelle wore a threadbare dress and fraying slippers. A shawl—the ratty one from before—was wrapped around her narrow shoulders. Her gaunt face was impossibly thin, the cheekbones threatening to poke through the skin.

"May we come in, Mrs. Whitlock?" Claire asked. Gavin's hand was discreetly on his weapon. He caught the meaning in the glance she'd given him. They would work as a team. She would distract Maribelle while he made sure Xavier wasn't hiding in the house.

The older woman waved her in. Claire crossed over the threshold. "Is someone here with you?"

"No." Maribelle wrapped the shawl tighter around her shoulders. The interior of the home wasn't any warmer than outside. A wooden stove sat unused in the center of the living room. "Xavier hasn't been here for days."

"Do you know where he is?"

She shook her head. Her gaze followed Gavin as he crossed to the opposite side of the room before settling back on Claire. "Xavier doesn't keep me informed about his whereabouts. You said there was news about Stephanie? What is it?"

"Let's sit down." Claire steered Stephanie's mother toward a scratched kitchen table. Maribelle looked ready to collapse on her feet. A pot of tea was steaming on the stove. Claire gathered a crack cup from the drying rack and poured some. She pushed it toward Maribelle with a gentle smile. "It's cold today."

"It is." She wrapped her hands around the mug. Her voice was hoarse as if rarely used. "Please, Sheriff...I need to know about my daughter."

Claire pulled out a chair and sat. There was no easy way to say this. "I'm so sorry, Mrs. Whitlock, but yesterday, we discovered your daughter's body inside her vehicle. She was murdered."

Maribelle blinked. Her chin trembled. "And the note?"

Claire set the postcard on the table. "We had this analyzed. Stephanie didn't write it."

Her hands tightened around the mug. Tears leaked from her eyes, but there was no shock or denial. Claire let out a breath. "You suspected she was dead?"

Maribelle nodded. "My daughter wouldn't have cut off communication with me. She didn't get along with Xavier. That's no secret, but we were very close." She nibbled her lip. "I'm sorry, Sheriff. Faye's death is my fault. Last month, she came to visit me in the hospital.

I'm sick. Heart failure. I asked her to look for Stephanie... I wanted my baby found."

"Why didn't you come to me with your suspicions?"

"I didn't think you would believe me. I figured if Faye tried to look for Stephanie, and couldn't find her, she would ask you to reopen the case."

Claire tamped down the anger threatening to flood her veins. Maribelle wasn't responsible for Faye's death, but she could've aided the investigation. They'd been on her front porch a week ago and she'd said nothing. But Xavier had been there. "Your husband didn't want you to look for Stephanie, did he?"

"No. Xavier..." She swallowed hard. "He's a difficult man. Stephanie didn't approve of the way he treated me. It caused many arguments. But he didn't kill my daughter, if that's what you're asking. Xavier was here with me the night that Stephanie disappeared."

Claire stilled. Was Maribelle lying? She could be protecting Xavier. "Can you be certain your husband had nothing to do with Stephanie's murder?"

"Absolutely. Xavier is capable of bad things, but he didn't kill Stephanie."

"Does he hurt you?"

Maribelle didn't answer. Her gaze was locked on the tea in front of her. Claire felt, rather than heard, Gavin standing near the front door. He was keeping guard, but not intruding on the conversation.

Claire placed a hand on Maribelle's arm. The bones were delicate and thin, like a bird. "If you want to leave Xavier, I can protect you. He won't harm you ever again."

"Where would I go? I have no money. I'm ill—"

"We can make arrangements. For starters, you can stay in a cabin on my family's property." She tilted her head to look Maribelle in the eye. "Let's get you someplace warm and then we can figure out the next steps."

Maribelle hesitated. "I won't answer questions about my husband, Sheriff. Or about the Chosen. It's a risk to leave here with you. Betraying Xavier any further would put me in serious danger."

"You're protected under the law, Mrs. Whitlock. I can't compel you to testify against your husband or answer my questions about him. You would have to waive your right of spousal privilege. I understand why you wouldn't."

The woman was terrified of her husband. Claire's immediate concern was getting Maribelle some place safe. But the older woman's statement confirmed Xavier was conducting illegal activity on his property. Did it also mean she was lying about where her husband was on the night of Stephanie's murder? It was possible. But Claire's gut said Maribelle was telling the truth. The love she had for her daughter was obvious. It seemed unlikely she would protect Stephanie's murderer, even if it meant risking her own life.

Maribelle placed her hand over Claire's and squeezed. "Faye said you were nice, that I could trust you. She was right."

Those kind words sent a wave of unexpected grief crashing through Claire. *Oh Faye, what I wouldn't give to speak to you now.* One last conversation...to say all the things she hadn't in life. It was a regret she'd carry with her forever. Claire had been in survival mode for so long, she'd forgotten how to express her feelings to those she loved.

Was she making the same mistake with Gavin? She hadn't told him how she truly felt. She was so busy trying to protect her heart, she hadn't shared what was in it.

Maribelle released Claire's hand and sat back in her chair. She licked her lips nervously. "I need to tell you something, but no one can know you found out about it from me. Please give me your word."

"You have it."

"My daughter was seeing someone secretly. She was in love, but I was concerned the young man didn't feel the same. That he was playing with my daughter's feelings. His family didn't approve of Stephanie." Maribelle's lips flattened into a thin line. "Then she ended up pregnant. Stephanie said she was getting married and then..."

She'd been killed. Claire's mind whirled with possibilities. She leaned forward. "Do you know who Stephanie was secretly dating?"

Maribelle nodded, lifting her gaze to meet Claire's. "Ian Scott, the mayor's son."

Gavin's hands tightened on the steering wheel as he maneuvered around a tractor stuttering along the two-lane country road. His mind raced as quickly as his tires rotated against the asphalt. He'd known there was something strange about their interactions with Ian Scott. Could he have killed his secret girlfriend when she became pregnant? Sadly, that type of scenario was far too common. Especially if Ian felt trapped between his family's expectations and Stephanie's.

He certainly had the clout to determine who the next sheriff would be. His father was the mayor and his wife worked for City Hall. Convincing them to hire someone Ian had selected would be a simple matter.

In the passenger seat beside him, Claire hung up her phone and tossed it in the cup holder. "Ian called in sick this morning, but no one is answering the phone at his house. His cell is turned off. Something about this isn't right."

"Do you think he'd run? We found Stephanie's body yesterday. Ian could be on a Mexican beach by now."

"I doubt it." She gripped the door handle as Gavin sped through a yellow light. "Ian wasn't honest with us about his relationship with Stephanie, but there could be several reasons why. We can't assume he's the killer."

Gavin tapped the brakes as he turned into Ian's neighborhood. Within moments, they parked in the mansion's driveway. The front door swung open and a female housekeeper in a black uniform rushed out. Her eyes were wide with fear. In one hand, she held a cell phone.

"Thank goodness you got here so quickly." The woman's words tumbled out. From the cell phone's speaker, a voice demanded answers. The housekeeper was on the phone with emergency services. Tears rolled down her face. "Mr. Scott has a gun. I don't know what he plans to do with it."

"Where is he?" Gavin barked out, his hand immediately flying to his own weapon.

"In his bedroom. I think he's been drinking. When I went in to clean, he screamed for me to stay away. I've never seen him so angry."

"Is anyone else in the house?" Claire asked. She'd palmed her own weapon.

"Kylie, the other housekeeper, is still upstairs. I tried to get her to come with me to call the police, but she wouldn't move..."

The rest of her sentence dissolved into sobs. She was shaking uncontrollably. Gavin ordered her to stay put and then quickly jogged up the walkway to the front door. It hung open. "Police, Mr. Scott. I'm coming in."

There was no reply. Claire appeared by his side, her tone sharp as she relayed instructions to dispatch. The radio crackled. Backup was ten minutes away.

A lot could happen in ten minutes. Ian was armed and possibly drunk. Killer or not, he wasn't acting rationally. There was an innocent woman still in the house. Gavin had to find her before she was harmed. He crossed the threshold, gun outstretched. The tiled entryway was empty. A spiral staircase led to the upper floor. Gavin's boots didn't make a sound as he ascended.

Claire stayed close, her own weapon raised. Near the landing, she whispered, "The housekeeper said the bedroom is at the end of the hall."

He was glad she'd had the presence of mind to ask

because Gavin hadn't. He adjusted the grip on his weapon. Sweat beaded along his hairline. He listened for any sound, but the house was quiet. The ornate double doors leading to the bedroom were shut. Thick carpeting sank under his feet and the hallway smelled of elderflower and whiskey.

Gavin slid alongside the bedroom doors. "Ian Scott, this is the police. Put your weapon down and come out with your hands up."

Silence. Gavin glanced at Claire as she reached for the door handle. Time seemed to stop as their gazes held. Adrenaline sharpened his senses, imprinting everything about Claire in his brain. The loose strand of hair curving around her neck, the smattering of freckles on her nose, the determination in her crystal blue eyes. Emotions Gavin couldn't name rolled through him like a hurricane. They threatened to unmoor him.

He was falling in love with her. Right or wrong, good timing or not, the truth smacked him clear across the face. There was no going back. He would lay down his life for this woman. Not because it was his job, but because his heart demanded it.

Lord, I don't know where you're leading me, but I'm trusting in You. Guide me. Keep us safe.

"Ready?" Claire whispered.

Gavin relaxed the iron grip on his weapon and then nodded sharply. She pushed on the handle. The door was unlocked. Sobs filtered into the hall from inside the bedroom. Claire shoved the door open fully and Gavin swung inside, gun raised.

It was a sitting area. Silk couches were arranged near a fireplace. Thick drapes, drawn tight, cast the entire room in shadows. The scent of whiskey grew stronger. Several empty bottles were scattered around the room.

A woman was crouched in the corner. The shoulders of her housekeeper's uniform shook with the force of her sobs. Cleaning supplies spilled across the carpet. Claire hurried over, crouching next to the housekeeper. Her voice was a whisper as she grasped the woman's arm and tugged her into a standing position.

Gavin kept moving, searching for Ian. Another set of double doors led to an interior room. A four-poster bed came into view. The covers were twisted, dangling off the mattress to skim the floor. A familiar noise reached Gavin's ears, but for a moment, he couldn't place what it was. Then it struck him. It was the sound of a barrel spinning. Was Ian playing Russian roulette?

Taking a deep breath to counteract the burst of fresh adrenaline, Gavin entered the bedroom. It was empty. Another door led to an office with wood paneling. Ian was seated at the desk. Clothes wrinkled and stained, he sported a full beard. His hair was wild, standing on end, as if he'd been running his hands through it. The stark light from the lamp cast menacing shadows on his face. A half-drunk bottle of whiskey sat at his elbow.

He held a pistol in one hand, pointed to his own temple.

Gavin lifted his own weapon. As long as Ian held a gun, he presented a danger to himself and others. It wasn't a risk to take lightly. "Mr. Scott, it's Texas Ranger

Gavin Sterling. Slowly put the gun down on the desk and raise your hands."

Ian's gaze lifted. His eyes were bloodshot. "No. I don't deserve to live. Stephanie's dead because of me."

Gavin's heart stuttered. He wanted to ask questions, but the priority was saving Ian's life. "Whatever happened, we can sort it out. I can help you—"

"Help me? You can't help me. I can't prove my father killed her. You won't be able to either. He's too smart for the both of us."

Shock reverberated through Gavin. His mind struggled to fit what he'd gathered about the case with Ian's accusation. "Put the gun down. Let's talk about it. We'll figure out a way to get justice for Stephanie."

"Dad was incensed when he found out I was dating her." Ian took a swig of whiskey, never lowering the gun from his temple. A tear leaked from one bloodshot eye, trailing a track down his cheek. "I loved Stephanie. We started seeing each other in secret, and suddenly, my entire world fell into place. She wasn't interested in my money or my last name. It was the first time in my life anyone cared about my dreams. I was going to marry her. We...we were going to have a family."

His face flushed as his tone turned hard. "But she didn't fit into the vision Dad had for me. The great Patrick Scott needs a family who can play the political game. A son to follow in his footsteps, with the perfect wife, and the experience to be a US senator."

Movement behind Ian caught Gavin's attention. Claire was visible through another open door leading into a hallway. Her gaze was locked on the mayor's son. She edged forward. What was she doing?

Ian laughed, but there was no mirth in it. "I hate politics. It's the last thing I want to do."

Gavin fixed his gaze on the man in front of him. "I need you to put the gun down now."

Ian ignored him, taking another swig of whiskey. "My dad confessed he'd offered Stephanie $100,000 to leave town and never speak to me again. He said she took the money." He rose from the chair, tension coiling his body. His face was mottled with rage. "That was a lie. All this time, I thought Stephanie betrayed me. Betrayed us. But she didn't. My father never gave her the money. He murdered her and buried her in the lake so no one would find out."

Claire took another step forward into the room. She was three paces from Ian. Gavin's chest tightened as he realized her intentions. She was attempting to disarm the man. It was reckless and extremely dangerous. Gavin tried to meet her gaze, but Claire's sole focus was on Ian.

"Put the gun down." Desperation bled into Gavin's voice. "There's no need to do this. You aren't responsible for Stephanie's death. She wouldn't want you to hurt yourself."

Ian swayed, seemingly to struggle with his emotions. "I didn't kill her, but I'm the reason Stephanie's dead. My sweet, sweet love..." Tears rolled down his cheeks. "I'm so sorry."

His finger slid to the trigger. Gavin took a step forward, but the desk blocked his path. "No, Ian!"

Claire leapt, flying through the air and tackling Ian. They collided with the desk. Items toppled over and the lamp shattered as it hit the edge. Gavin made a grab for Ian and missed. The mayor's son and Claire slid to the floor, a tangle of arms and legs.

The gun fired.

FIFTEEN

Claire pressed an ice pack to her bruised forearm. She rammed it against the unyielding desk in her scuffle with Ian. The hospital's emergency room reception area was buzzing with activity. Ambulances came and went in a steady stream, paramedics rushing patients past the giant doors leading to the exam rooms. Half an hour ago, Ian was hurried threw those same doors, bleeding from a gunshot graze to the scalp. But he was alive. Claire was grateful.

Across the room, Gavin turned away from the coffee machine, holding two cups. His long strides ate up the distance between them. Butterflies rioted in Claire's stomach. The man was a distraction she didn't need but couldn't escape. How was it possible they'd only been working together for several days? It felt like a lifetime.

He set the coffee cups on a nearby table. "How's your arm?"

"It's fine. Just bruised." She tried for levity. "Remind me not to smash into any more desks, will you?"

His lips curved into a smile, but it didn't reach his eyes. Gavin's strong fingers wrapped around her wrist. His palm was warm. He gently tugged the ice pack away from her elbow. His gaze swept over the injury, causing a burst of heat to blaze through her veins. "It's swollen. Are you sure you don't want to have that x-rayed?"

"I'm sure. It'll be a wonderful shade of purple tomorrow, but I'll survive."

He didn't release her wrist. Instead, he stepped closer, his gaze lifting to her face. An emotion she couldn't quite place was buried in his eyes. It made her breath catch. The bustle of the room faded away.

"You scared me, Claire. That move isn't one they teach in the academy. What on earth were you thinking?"

"Saving Ian's life. It's why we're in this job, right? To protect people, even from themselves sometimes."

He sighed, then leaned forward to brush his lips across her forehead. It was tender. Sweet. Claire leaned into the touch, wrapping her uninjured arm around his narrow waist. The familiar scent of his aftershave calmed her racing mind. Gavin's lips brushed against her hair. The steady beat of his heart thumped against her ear.

Claire wanted to sink into his embrace and never let go. But that wasn't possible. There was unfinished business between them. Now wasn't the time to address it, but it had to be soon. Her heart couldn't take much more of this.

She released Gavin under the guise of picking up her

coffee. She took a sip and winced. "Yikes. They should put a warning sign on that machine. Drink this if you don't want any stomach lining left."

He arched his brows. "You're spoiled by that fancy machine in the sheriff department's break room."

"Yes, I am. What's the point of being in charge if I can't have decent coffee?"

They both laughed. Through the large glass windows overlooking the parking lot, Claire spotted the mayor marching up the walkway to the entrance. Heather, Ian's wife, hurried after him in sky-high heels. Her designer purse banged against her thigh.

Claire jutted her chin toward the door. "They're here."

Gavin turned, gaze narrowing. Claire straightened her uniform shirt. This conversation had to be handled carefully. If Ian's accusation was correct, Mayor Patrick Scott was a killer. But they had no hard evidence implicating him. Claire needed to ask questions, but she didn't want Patrick to realize he was a suspect. Not yet.

She also had to consider that Ian could be lying. He might've killed Stephanie after learning she'd accepted his father's money. Love and hate were often two sides of the same coin, and betrayal could turn deadly.

The main door swished open. Patrick's gaze swept the waiting room, zeroing in on Claire as she moved to intercept him. His face was flushed, his suit jacket hanging open, tie askew. "What on earth happened? Where is my son?"

Heather joined them. She was faintly out of breath,

her shoulders turned inward, and complexion pale. "Is he all right?"

"Ian will be fine." Claire pitched her voice low. "He's suffered a minor injury, but should recover. He's with the doctors now. Please come with me so we can discuss what happened."

She led the way to a conference room. A large table took up the center of the room, surrounded by faux leather chairs. The scent of stale pizza lingered in the space. Claire waited for everyone to traipse inside, and then closed the door behind her. She took a deep breath. "Ian attempted to commit suicide."

Heather sank into the nearest chair, hugging her purse to her chest. She appeared stunned.

Color rose in Patrick's cheeks, and he crossed his arms over his chest. "That's preposterous. I will not tolerate you lying about my son. First that horrible newspaper article and now this."

"Stop right there." Gavin's tone brooked no argument. "Claire isn't lying. In fact, she saved your son's life. You should be thanking her."

Patrick's mouth popped open and then shut again. His jaw worked. Heather placed a reassuring hand on his arm. "You have to forgive the mayor. He loves his son deeply, and this news is disturbing to us both. It's difficult to wrap our minds around."

"Heather's right." Patrick shook his head. "Why on earth would Ian attempt suicide?"

"He was distressed over Stephanie Madden's murder." Claire kept her attention locked on the mayor.

"Are you aware, sir, that your son and Stephanie had a secret relationship?"

Heather paled further, but there was no flicker of surprise in her expression. She'd known about the relationship. Or at least suspected. Claire remembered Heather had been standing next to the mayor in the photograph taken at the campaign event. The same picture that caught Ian and Stephanie flirting.

Patrick stiffened slightly. "Yes, I was aware of their relationship, but they broke up before her death."

"Ian says you paid Stephanie $100,000 dollars to leave town and never speak to him again. Is that true?"

Heather's eyes widened, but she remained silent. Claire could practically see the wheels turning in her head. She was wondering where they were going with this.

"I did what was necessary to protect my son." Patrick jutted up his chin. "Stephanie was after his money. I knew it from the beginning, but Ian was...foolish. He couldn't see the wicked woman for what she truly was. Manipulative. I offered her cash, and she took it."

"Hold on." Gavin pitched forward. "You gave Stephanie $100,000 *in cash?*"

"I did. The day before she left town, as a matter of fact."

None of the money had been found, either in Stephanie's vehicle nor at her house. Claire had spoken to her extended family members personally. Stephanie hadn't owned much. Her bank account, at the time of her death, had three hundred dollars in it.

So what happened to the cash?

Patrick's brow furrowed. "Sheriff King knew all about this. I told him myself. It's part of the reason he believed Stephanie left town."

Anger washed over Claire and it took everything inside her to keep from balling her hands into fists. Randy King purposefully left out pertinent information in his case file and when they spoke to him on his farm. To protect the Scott family. Claire wasn't surprised—Sheriff King and Mayor Scott were old friends—but his decision infuriated her all the same. He'd put people's lives at risk. Gavin's. Her son's.

She would deal with Randy King, but at the moment, Claire had bigger issues. She took a deep breath to temper her anger so it wouldn't bleed into her voice. "When did you tell Ian about giving Stephanie the money?"

"After she left town." His gaze skipped between Claire and Gavin. "I fail to see why these questions are relevant."

"They're trying to prove Ian murdered Stephanie." Heather's tone was hard. Her ruby lips flattened into a thin line and hatred seemed to seep from her pores as she stared Claire down.

A cold finger of doubt crept down Claire's spine as a memory bubbled to the surface. Ian wasn't the only one who lied about his relationship with Stephanie. Heather had too.

Patrick straightened. "I told you, my son had nothing to do with Stephanie's murder."

There was a ring of sincerity in his words. Patrick could be telling the truth. Or he could be protecting his son at any costs. It was time to hit the mayor with some evidence and see where that got her.

"Two years ago, about a week before Stephanie's murder, you filed a police report notifying authorities that a handgun had been stolen from your home. We've found the weapon. Can you explain how it ended up buried with Stephanie in her car at the bottom of the lake?"

Patrick's expression hardened, and he adjusted his suit jacket as if he was going to battle. "Clearly, there were details missing from the police report. That handgun was stored next to my bedside in an unlocked drawer. I noticed it missing after I had a campaign event in my home. Half of Fulton County attended. Anyone could've stolen it."

Gavin's brows arched. "A guest in your home went upstairs, into your bedroom, and stole a handgun? That's very specific. Was anything else taken?"

"Some of my late wife's jewelry. I don't suppose you recovered any of that in Stephanie's car?"

His tone was sarcastic, and it grated on Claire's patience. This wasn't a joke or a game. "The missing jewelry wasn't listed among the stolen items."

He shrugged. "The deputy must've forgotten to include it."

"I've had enough of this." Heather's posture straightened as heat colored her cheeks. "Ian didn't murder anyone and I can prove it. Sheriff, you believe the same person killed Stephanie and Faye. Well, we were all having dinner together—Ian, the mayor, and I—at my home on the night Faye died. My chef made salmon."

Patrick placed a hand on Heather's shoulder. "She's right. Ian and I were speaking about our family's grocery business for hours afterward. I was with him until well after midnight. Talk to the head housekeeper. She'll tell you the same." He arched a brow, as if challenging them to argue. "In the meantime, if you have any other questions, contact my attorney. We need to check on Ian."

Heather rose. She gripped her bag with one hand. "Sheriff. Ranger Sterling."

Patrick escorted his daughter-in-law to the door. He waited until she crossed over the threshold before turning back to face Claire. "Thank you for saving my son, Sheriff. You've done a good deed for my family today, so I'm going to give you a piece of advice. You're skating a thin line. Don't make an enemy of me. It won't bode well for you."

Beside her, Gavin stiffened. Claire held the mayor's gaze, despite the tangle of dread curling in her stomach. "I told you when this case started, I will see it through to the end. No one—including you—will stop me from doing my job."

Patrick's glare could melt glaciers. He spun around and left the room, slamming the door behind him.

SIXTEEN

Gavin hung up his phone, frustration nipping at him. "I hate to say it, but Mayor Scott was right. Ryker interviewed the head housekeeper. According to her, the family had dinner together on the night Faye was murdered. Heather had a headache and went to bed early. Mayor Scott and Ian discussed business in the study until eleven thirty. The housekeeper was in and out of the room frequently, bringing drinks and additional food. The mayor left around eleven thirty. Neither man could've killed Faye."

Claire was silent for a long moment. She stood in front of the whiteboard, studying the timeline and crime scene photos. The noise from the deputies beyond the glass walls of her office filtered in. Keith, Claire's chief deputy, rose from his desk and disappeared into the break room. Probably for coffee. Gavin was tempted to grab a cup for himself. It'd been an emotionally draining day and his energy was waning.

"This doesn't make sense," Claire said, drawing Gavin's attention back to her. She'd changed into a fresh uniform after the hospital. The crisp creases and polished badge matched the determination in her voice. "Every one of our suspects has an alibi for at least one of the murders. Either someone is lying or—"

Claire inhaled sharply and her eyes widened. "There's more than one person involved. We could be looking at two killers, working together."

All thoughts of caffeine fled as a jolt of adrenaline shot through Gavin's veins. "That's an interesting thought."

"It's something I've been pondering for a while. Stephanie's car was pulled into the lake using a boat. It's technically possible that one person could accomplish it, but it makes a lot more sense if two people are involved."

"One person ambushed Stephanie at her house, took her to the lake by force, and shot her. The other drove the boat to the meeting place and helped drag the vehicle into the water." Gavin pictured the scenario in his mind. "You're right. It makes sense with two people involved. But we don't have any evidence to support the theory. It's just supposition."

"I know. Let's run with the idea anyway and see where it gets us."

"I'm game."

Claire tapped her fingers against her lips. Gavin enjoyed watching her think. Most of their time together had been spent working the case. What would it be like to hang out on the lake with Jacob and fish? Or share a candlelight dinner together before snuggling on the couch with a movie? He wanted to find out.

Had he messed everything up by being honest with Claire about his fears? Gavin didn't know. And now wasn't the time to ask. Claire had enough problems on her plate. After the case was over, when she had some time to grieve Faye, then he'd see where they stood.

Claire dropped her hand. "Do you believe Ian is telling the truth about his father?"

"I do. At least...I'm convinced Ian believes his father killed Stephanie. He was extremely drunk when he gave us that information. It could've been a ploy to cast suspicion on someone else, but there are much easier ways to accomplish that. And I don't doubt Ian was going to pull the trigger today. He'd be dead if you hadn't tackled him." Gavin pointed to a photograph of the Glock taken from Stephanie's car. "Then there's the murder weapon to consider. Patrick's story about the gun being stolen from his home is possible, but it's also unlikely."

"Agreed. Okay, let's put together what we know. Patrick discovered his son was having a secret relationship with Stephanie. He didn't approve. He offered Stephanie money to leave Ian alone...what if she refused it?"

"That would infuriate Patrick." Gavin leaned against the conference table. "But there's one problem. In the days before Stephanie's murder, Patrick removed $100,000 from his bank account. We have records proving it."

Claire lifted her gaze to meet his. "That's where the accomplice comes in."

He inhaled sharply. "It was a payoff."

"Yep. According to her mother, Stephanie was pregnant. She and Ian were planning to elope. The mayor didn't have time to waste. He had to get rid of Stephanie quickly. He makes a plan to kill her. Patrick files a police report listing his gun as stolen and then pulls money out of his bank account." Her gaze swept across the board. "He hires someone to help kill Stephanie. The question is, who was he working with?"

"It has to be someone he trusts."

"What if it's Heather?"

Gavin's mouth dropped open. Claire could've said Santa Claus was the mayor's accomplice and he would've been less shocked. "What?"

"She lied to us about her relationship with Stephanie. Why would Heather do that if there was nothing to hide? Then it occurred to me...she had as much to lose as Patrick did. Remember the photograph of Ian and Stephanie at the park? Heather was there, in the picture, standing next to the mayor. And she was as angry as he was. Heather may have already been in love with Ian, even back then."

"But to commit murder over it? That's a stretch."

"Not when you think about what Ian told us at the country club. His father pushed him to marry Heather." Claire ran a hand over her ponytail. "They could've made an agreement. Both of them wanted Stephanie gone. People have killed for a lot less."

Gavin had to admit Claire made a good argument. But they were low on evidence. "Even if that's true, we don't have a way to prove it. Not yet."

A knock at the office door cut off Claire's response. When she called out for the person to enter, Keith poked his head inside the door. "Randy King is here to see you, ma'am. He says it's urgent."

"I bet he did," she muttered. Claire flipped the whiteboard to the blank side, hiding their notes about the murders. "Show him in."

Keith disappeared. Gavin arched his brows. "What does Sheriff King want?"

"To lecture me. I'm sure he was the first call Mayor Scott made when he left the hospital this afternoon." She straightened her shoulders and marched behind her desk. "I'm glad Sheriff King showed up. I have a few things of my own to say."

Gavin positioned himself near the credenza. He was close enough to make his presence known, but far enough away to allow Claire to lead the conversation. This was her battle. One, as much as Gavin hated to acknowledge, she had to fight on her own. Otherwise, Sheriff King and her subordinates wouldn't respect the boundary lines she drew.

Randy appeared in the doorway. The former sheriff was dressed like a ranch hand in a fringe leather jacket and scuffed boots. Dark circles hung low under his eyes. He carried a notebook in one hand. Without asking, he entered and shut the door behind him. "We need to talk."

"We certainly do." Claire's tone was polite, but there

was a hidden edge of anger lining it. She crossed her arms over her chest. "For starters, I'd like to know why you've been keeping relevant information about Stephanie Madden's case secret. You're a private citizen now, Sheriff King, but you served this community for decades. I'd hoped that meant something. It clearly doesn't."

His shoulders rolled inward, as if her words were poisonousness darts. "It does mean something. I owe you an apology, Claire. I believed Stephanie had left town on her own accord."

"She didn't."

He sank into a visitor's chair. "My wife and I took a trip to Fort Worth. I accidentally left my cell behind at the house. I only found out you'd discovered Stephanie's body when I returned late last night. I immediately started looking for this."

He lifted the notebook in his hand. "It's my personal diary. I often wrote notes and observations about cases I was working on. You should read it. It'll help with your investigation."

It was awful, but Gavin questioned Randy's change of heart. The man seemed sincere, but could he be trusted? Claire must've had the same thoughts, because her gaze narrowed and she asked, "Mayor Scott hasn't called you?"

"He did. I share his concern that you're headed down the wrong path with this investigation. Ian didn't kill Stephanie." Randy set the notebook down on her desk. "You need to take a closer look at Alex Sheffield."

"Why?"

"Because he's not the person he claims to be. Alex belongs to the Chosen. He has a tattoo on the inside of his arm."

Gavin stiffened. "You knew Alex was a member of the Chosen and you're just now telling us?"

"I didn't know it was relevant until Stephanie turned up dead. Xavier is still missing, right?" Randy waited for Gavin to nod before continuing. "He may not be alive anymore. If the rumors are true, Alex challenged Xavier for a leadership position in the group. It failed. Since then, he's been towing the line, but this may have been the opportunity he needs to frame someone else for crimes he committed. Starting with Stephanie's murder. She betrayed him by dating Ian. When Alex found out, he was furious."

"How do you know all of this?" Claire asked.

"As you pointed out, I was sheriff for decades. Witnesses and conversations are all listed in the notebook." Randy glanced at Gavin and then focused back on Claire. "Learn from my mistakes. Follow the evidence, Sheriff, and ignore everything else."

Claire wrapped the ends of her oversized cardigan around her midsection. It was late, and although her body was exhausted, her mind wouldn't shut off. Dishes rattled in the kitchen as Gavin cleaned up after dinner. She'd offered to help, but he insisted on doing it himself. There was something comforting about his steady presence in her home.

Thunder lit up the night sky. The white flash illuminated the lake and woods behind her house. There was another storm coming. In more ways than one. Since discovering Stephanie's body in the lake, Claire had the overwhelming sense that the killer wasn't done with her. Not yet.

It was an awful feeling she couldn't shake.

After the conversation with Sheriff King, she'd read every page of his notebook. Most of it was based on innuendo and rumors, but it all had to be looked into. The Texas Rangers sprang into action, dividing up the witnesses, and attempting to track down more evidence that would lead them to the killer. Or killers.

There was nothing more to do. Not tonight. She reached for the leather-bound Bible on the end table beside the couch and flipped to the homemade bookmark tucked within the pages. Faye had gifted it to Claire. The intricately cross-stitched birds were accompanied by a verse.

Be strong and courageous. Do not be afraid; do not be discouraged, for the Lord your God will be with you wherever you go.

A sense of peace swept over Claire. It was the reminder she needed, especially tonight.

Gavin came around the corner. A water stain spread across his shirt and the fabric clung to his chest muscles. He carried a steaming mug in one hand. "I made you a cup of tea. If you're lucky, it's drinkable. That fancy kettle has more buttons than mission control."

She chuckled. He was right. The kettle had six different temperature settings for perfect brewing along with a stay warm function. It'd been a gift from her parents when she moved in. Claire set her Bible down before accepting the mug Gavin offered. Their fingers brushed, sending a jolt of electricity up her arm. "I'm the tea is wonderful. Thank you."

"You're welcome." His gaze dropped to the Bible. He picked up the bookmark, running his fingers over the delicately stitched verse. "Did you make this?"

"Faye did. Jacob was only six weeks old and my divorce had just been finalized when a gift showed up in the mail. Baby clothes and other things, along with this bookmark. The verse was her favorite."

It was one Claire didn't always live by. She hadn't with Gavin. The fear of being hurt had held her back from saying what was in her heart, but she couldn't remain silent anymore. It was time to be courageous.

Please, God, give me the right words.

She set her tea down on the coffee table and turned to face the man seated on the couch next to her. She took his hand. "Gavin, there's something I need to say. I've been thinking a lot about our conversation in the hospital."

"Claire..." He ran a thumb across her knuckle, sending a sweet wave of warmth coursing through her. "I don't mind having this conversation tonight, but there's no need. We can talk another time—"

"No. We've been shot at, chased, and nearly blown up. Before some other catastrophe happens, I need to say this." She took a deep breath. "You aren't the only one who fears not being good enough. I was married once. It ended in disaster. My husband cheated on me, left me while I was pregnant, and moved to the other side of the world without a backward glance. Starting a new relationship...it's the last thing I ever thought about doing. And then you walked into my life."

Tenderness softened the hard planes of his face. Gavin's hand cupped her cheek, his fingers threading through the strands of her hair. His touch was irresistible. And oh, that look in his eyes. She wanted to melt in it.

Claire gave into her desire and laid her head on his broad chest. "You make me want to try, Gavin. With you, things could be different. But I can't do this alone. I learned that the hard way in my marriage. I can't convince you. You have to believe in us—in the love we could have—on your own."

"You're right. I do." He tightened his arms around her and brushed a kiss across her temple. "I've been thinking a lot too. I'm not the same man I was when my ex and I broke up. God wasn't a part of my life then. But He is now and my faith...it changes things. The first day we were working on this case, I said God had brought me here for a reason. I thought it was to protect you. Now I realize He had bigger plans for me. For us."

Claire's pulse jumped. Was he saying what she thought he was saying?

"Maybe the key is to love each other, keep communication open, and to hand our fears over to the Lord." Gavin gently grasped her chin and tilted it upward until she was looking him in the face. "I'm falling in love with you, Claire. You and Jacob. I'm not going anywhere as long you'll both have me."

Her breath caught. His speech was the most romantic thing anyone had ever said to her. Tears pricked Claire's eyes as her heart burst wide open. Gavin searched her face, a faint hint of worry lurking in his chestnut eyes. "Did I say too much?"

Claire swallowed past the lump in her throat. "No. You said everything perfectly." She leaned in closer, her lips brushing against his in a gentle kiss. "I'm falling in love with you too."

He inhaled sharply and his hand trembled slightly as he tilted her head to deepen the kiss. Claire lost herself in the moment. She was safe with Gavin. There would be bumps along the road during their romance, but she knew with every ounce of her being that he would never purposefully hurt her. She could trust him with her heart.

When the kiss ended, they were both breathless. Gavin pulled her back into the circle of his arms. Claire rested her head on his chest, snuggling into the comfort of his embrace. They stayed like that for a long time, not talking, just enjoying the quiet moment together. Rain tapped against the windowpane.

Finally, Gavin sighed. "It's late. I should go. We have a meeting first thing tomorrow morning with the entire ranger team."

Reality came crashing down on Claire like a bucket of icy water. Things with Gavin were settled, but the case wasn't over. They were no closer to finding the killer —or killers—than they had been this morning.

"Can we talk the crimes through again, one more time?" Claire backed away from Gavin to look him in the face. "I feel like we're missing something. Something obvious. It's right there at the edge of my mind, but I can't grasp it."

"Sure—"

Claire's cell phone cut him off. She ran to the kitchen to grab it from the charger. The number wasn't one she recognized. "Sheriff Wilson."

"Someone's here." Maribelle's voice was hushed and ladened with fear. "It's Xavier. He broke into my cabin —" A sob choked off her words.

Claire flew into motion, pulling on her shoes. Gavin appeared by her side and she put the call on speaker. "I'm coming right now. Keep talking to me, Maribelle. Can you get out of the cabin?"

"No. I'm hiding in the closet. But I can hear him searching. Hurry, please! He's going to find me, and when he does...he'll kill me."

SEVENTEEN

Gavin raced through the trees separating Claire's cabin from Maribelle's. Rain pelted his head, the water running in rivets down the back of his collar to chill his skin. Branches tugged at his clothes. His breath came in puffs, the frigid air shocking his lungs. Beside him, Claire kept pace. Her weapon was drawn and ready.

The cabin's lights were on. The back door swung open in the wind before slamming shut again, as if by an invisible hand. Pieces of the knob were scattered on the concrete. Xavier must've broken it while forcing his way inside. Gavin positioned himself next to the door, his boots sliding from the mud trapped in their treads.

Claire peeked in a window. Her wet hair was plastered to her head. She wasn't wearing a coat. Mud spatters painted her tennis shoes and the bottoms of her yoga pants. She dipped down next to Gavin, the scent of her citrus perfume mixing with the smell of the rain. "I don't see anyone in the living room."

Gavin adjusted his hold on the weapon in his hand. His gaze skimmed the road leading to the cabin. Where was the trooper assigned to watch the property? He should be here by now. They'd called for backup before leaving Claire's house.

"I don't like this." It felt like they were walking into a trap.

A scream came from inside. It was terror-filled and shrill. A fresh wave of adrenaline burst through Gavin's veins as the sound suddenly cut off. He sprang to his feet. There was no choice. Trap or no trap, they had to go in.

He grabbed the broken back door and burst into the house, gun raised. "Police! Put your weapons down and your hands in the air!"

Sounds came from the rear of the cabin. A man's voice was yelling, but Gavin couldn't make out the words. He raced across the tiny living room toward the hallway. Through the open door of the bedroom, he saw Xavier standing over Maribelle, beating her with the butt of a gun.

"Police!" Gavin shouted, aiming his weapon at the criminal. "Freeze!"

Xavier whirled, his own weapon raised. Gavin shoved Claire to the side just as a bullet flew into the molding near his head. Several more bullets followed. A fiery blaze streaked into Gavin's shoulder and he cried out as his hand went numb. His weapon clattered to the floor.

Warmth ran down his arm as blood bloomed on his shirt. He'd been shot. Claire grabbed him and pulled him farther out of range. Gavin shook off her aid. There wasn't time. He scooped up his weapon and held it with his left hand. He wasn't proficient at shooting with his weaker hand by any measure, but being unarmed wasn't an option.

Claire positioned herself near the hallway. "Xavier, put your gun down and your hands in the air! Now!"

Where was their backup? Something must've happened to the trooper. That thought terrified Gavin. Ryker was on his way with more law enforcement officers, but they were likely still several minutes away.

Maribelle moaned. The sound of flesh hitting flesh echoed. Claire's face flushed, but the hand holding her weapon was steady. Gavin peeked around the corner to see Xavier holding his wife up as a shield. Her head lolled. She was bleeding badly from a wound on her scalp.

Xavier raised his gun, pointing it at Claire. "Stay back. I ain't going to prison, Sheriff."

Oh yes, you are. Gavin gritted his teeth. It was either prison or Xavier was going to meet his maker. There were only two ways out of this situation.

"We can discuss it when you put your weapon down."

He laughed. It sounded manic and desperate. "How stupid do you think I am?" Xavier stepped back into the bedroom, dragging Maribelle with him. She moaned, and he gripped her tighter, shaking her slightly. "Who is setting me up, you dumb cow? Who is it?"

What was he talking about? Gavin cleared the

thought from his mind, along with the pain of his gunshot wound, and took aim. If he could just...

Xavier shifted, and the moment was gone. Sweat dripped into Gavin's eyes. He didn't have a clear shot, but there was more than one way to solve that problem. He locked eyes with Claire, pointed at Xavier, and then pointed at the door. She gave a sharp nod of agreement. The worry in her blue eyes nearly undid him. It wasn't for herself. For him.

Somewhere in the back corner of his mind, Gavin realized an additional weight rested on his shoulders. Every decision he made from here on out affected Claire. It wouldn't stop him from doing his job—protecting others was his purpose—but it was a deep responsibility to carry someone else's heart. And a blessing.

Gavin bolted for the back door. Pain punched his arm with every step. He ignored it. Outside, the icy rain numbed his wound. The thunderstorm slowed to a brisk drizzle. Lightning lit up the sky. He raced around the corner of the cabin and approached the bedroom window. Xavier was screaming something at Claire. It didn't make sense. Something about being framed.

Shivers racked Gavin's body as he took aim. He forced his muscles to stop and held his breath. Everything faded away as the world narrowed to the man in front of him. Gavin didn't relish shooting someone, but he would do what was necessary to save lives. He pulled the trigger.

Glass shattered as the bullet flew through the window and slammed into Xavier's back. Maribelle gave a short scream as the couple tumbled to the ground. Claire rushed into the room, gun drawn. She kicked Xavier's weapon away from his still fingers. Gavin tossed his handcuffs to her before clambering through the window. Shards of glass sliced at his palm.

Maribelle was tucked into a corner, moaning. Gavin approached her. "It's okay now. You're safe."

She sobbed and grabbed his arm. He comforted the older woman, glancing over Maribelle's head toward Claire. She had her fingers on Xavier's throat, checking for a pulse. "He's alive."

Relief rippled through Gavin. He didn't regret taking the shot, but he was thankful it hadn't ended Xavier's life. He fumbled to remove his phone from his pocket but couldn't make his injured fingers work. Maribelle was crying, lost in her own world, her gaze focused on something only she could see. She was going into shock. That was deadly. They needed paramedics. Now.

Claire whipped the sheet off the bed and pushed it against Xavier's gunshot wound. "Gavin, come hold this while I call for help."

He did as she asked. The sheet turned red with Xavier's blood. His hands were cuffed behind his back, and he remained unconscious. Gavin's head spun as the adrenaline wore off and the throbbing of his wound increased. He glanced at his shirt. It was saturated at the shoulder, but it didn't look like the bullet had hit anything major.

Claire tucked her phone against her ear. She took another sheet and ripped it with her teeth. Wrapping the bandage around Gavin's arm, she pulled tight as she spouted off commands to dispatch. Keith's voice came on the line. His tone was frantic, but his words weren't clear. Gavin leaned in closer.

Claire froze. The phone dropped from her ear as she whirled. Without a word, she raced from the room. Gavin yelled her name and then scooped up the phone. "Keith, what happened?"

"An emergency call was made from her parents' house. They're under attack."

The house was on fire.

Claire's heart thundered in her chest as she raced toward the flames. The entire living room was ablaze, smoke belching from the broken windows. Arson. Probably a Molotov cocktail, maybe two. There was no other explanation for how the fire could spread so quickly during a rainstorm.

Panic rippled through her. Where was Jacob? Her parents? Visions of every horrible scenario flashed through her mind. *No, God, no.* She put more fuel into her legs, wishing Gavin was with her. The memory of him screaming her name as she ran from Maribelle's cabin echoed in her mind. But there hadn't been time to explain. Besides, he'd been shot. The injury was serious enough to slow him down, even if he'd wanted to help.

Thinking of Gavin made her knees weak. His

shoulder had been bleeding badly. What if...No, she couldn't go down that road.

Raindrops coated her face and dripped into her eyes. Her tennis shoes slipped in the mud and she hit the ground hard on one knee. Pain ricocheted through her thigh. Claire shoved herself to a standing position and kept moving.

The back door to the house flew open. Smoke poured out and two figures appeared. It took Claire a moment to recognize her mother and father. A bruise and dried blood painted Lindsey's temple. Daniel had one arm thrown over his wife's shoulders. His other hand clutched his side. Blood stained his shirt. He took another step and collapsed on the patio, nearly taking Lindsey down with him.

"Dad!" Chest heaving, Claire joined her parents. She bent down to grab her father's arm. Together with Lindsey, they got him on his feet. Instinctively, Claire knew her mother was headed for the truck sitting in the driveway. Daniel needed a hospital. They headed in that direction.

"There's no time." Daniel's voice was hoarse as he tried to shake off Claire's help. "He has Jacob."

Claire's world tilted and spun. "Who?"

"We don't know. Someone threw bombs through the window and set the house on fire. I tried to stop him and was shot. He ripped Jacob straight from your mother's arms."

Tears poured down Lindsey's face, mixing with the soot and blood. Based on her mother's injuries, she fought to keep hold of Jacob. It was a miracle the intruder hadn't shot her too.

Claire didn't stop moving. She opened the passenger side of the truck and shoved her dad inside. "Which direction did the attacker go in?"

"Toward the dock."

She didn't think. Slamming the truck door, Claire spun toward the lake. It was a dark shadow. The long dock extending into the water wasn't visible, the moon obscured by the thunderstorm's cloud cover. She took off.

Jacob, hold on, baby. I'm coming.

Her heart said prayers even as her mind focused on rescuing her child. Her eyes adjusted to the darkness. The dock came into view. A boat bobbed on the water, secured by a rope to a mooring pole. Claire ducked into the tree line. She couldn't save Jacob by acting recklessly. Now was the time to rely on her training.

Moving closer, using the trees as cover, her gaze swept the area. A small form lying in the middle of the dock caught her attention. Jacob! He was motionless.

Dead? Her heart threatened to splinter in two. No, it couldn't be. She forced the devastating thought aside and focused on the task at hand. Getting to her son.

There was no way to reach him without exposing herself. Claire knew it was a trap. A sniper with a night vision scope would have no trouble killing her. There could be one on the boat. She should wait for backup. It had to be moments away. But what if Jacob was injured? Bleeding out? It was a risk Claire wasn't willing to take.

She burst from the tree line, keeping her head up, searching for any potential danger. Her feet pounded against the wooden dock. The injury from her earlier fall throbbed. She counted the distance in heartbeats, anticipating the crack of a gun followed by the fire of a bullet blazing through her. Jacob came into sharper focus. His eyes were closed.

Claire dropped to her knees beside him. Her fingers were numb from the cold. She couldn't tell if Jacob was breathing. The memory of finding Faye on the side of the road flashed in her mind. *No, please, no.*

With a shaking hand, she touched the smooth column of Jacob's throat. A steady beat thumped against her fingers. Alive. He was alive. Tears coursed down her cheeks. "Thank you, God."

There was no way to carry Jacob while holding her gun. Claire shoved it into the back of her pants and slipped her hands under her son. Lifting him into her arms, she leaned on her knees in preparation to stand, ignoring the screaming pain from her swelling knee. They needed to get off this dock.

A noise scraped against the dock one second before the barrel of a gun pushed against the back of Claire's head. She froze.

"Hello, Sheriff. I've been waiting for you."

EIGHTEEN

The trooper had been shot and left for dead.

Gavin used gauze from a first aid kit in the patrol car to staunch the wound. Smoke and flames poured from Claire's childhood home. Her parents were gone. It'd taken eight minutes for two deputies to arrive at Maribelle's cabin. Every second had been torture. Gavin couldn't leave until they arrived. He had a duty to keep Xavier in custody and to provide first aid to Maribelle.

And now...he had no idea where Claire or her family were.

The trooper groaned at the pressure applied to his injury. His eyes fluttered but didn't open. It wouldn't be possible for him to tell Gavin anything.

Footsteps came from the other side of the patrol car. Gavin whirled, raising his weapon. He found himself face-to-face with the barrel of a gun. Relief flooded through him when he recognized the man holding the weapon. Ryker.

The ranger rushed to Gavin's side. "What happened?"

"I don't know." Gavin lowered his weapon as Keith circled the vehicle. "Keith, take over providing first aid. I need to find Claire and her family."

The chief deputy knelt and grabbed more gauze from the first aid kit. "Claire's mother called. She's racing to the hospital. Daniel was shot and Jacob kidnapped. Claire went in pursuit. Last thing she knows, Claire was headed for the dock."

Gavin bolted to his feet. The gunshot wound sent white-hot agony racing down his nerve endings. Gritting his teeth against the pain, Gavin broke into a run, heading for the lake. He barely heard Keith shout, "More deputies are coming. Five minutes out."

Ryker fell into place beside him without a word, gun in hand. The heat from the blaze eating the log cabin faded as they raced for the dock. A boat—similar to the one the intruder had escaped in on the night of the bombing—was pulling away from the mooring pole.

Claire and Jacob were on it. There was no question in Gavin's mind.

"The boathouse." He deviated from the path to race for the building. Claire's father owned boats for his business and had moved several into the newly secured boathouse. Gavin's head swam, and he stumbled. Ryker caught him before he hit the ground.

"I'm driving the boat," Ryker said.

"Good idea." Gavin didn't intend for the rescue to turn into a suicide mission. He brushed off Ryker's aid and kept running. At the boathouse door, he punched in the code. The two men boarded one of the vessels quickly and fired up the engine. Every movement took time, precious seconds that Claire and Jacob were in danger, but there was no way to move faster.

Be strong and courageous. Do not be afraid; do not be discouraged, for the Lord your God will be with you wherever you go.

The biblical verse popped into Gavin's mind. It was a reminder that Claire and Jacob were not alone. Neither was he. They had God and He would be with them every step of the way.

Please, Lord. This couldn't be how their story ended. Gavin and Claire were falling in love. And Jacob...it was unthinkable to lose him. Gavin shoved the bleak thoughts from his mind and focused on his prayer. *Help me find them in time, Lord. You sent them to me. You opened my heart. Please don't take them from me now.*

Ryker pushed the throttle and increased their speed. Icy wind tore through the thin layer of Gavin's clothing. The lake was choppy from the thunderstorm and rain pelted the roof. He clung to the dash as they bounced over the surface. Every jolt sent agony through his shoulder.

"Where are they?" Ryker yelled the words to be heard over the rain and wind. "Do you see the boat?"

Gavin scanned the lake, panic clawing at his last thread of control. They were too late.

The boat carrying Claire and Jacob was gone.

Claire twisted her hands, attempting to free her wrists from their bonds. The zip ties dug into her skin. Warmth trickled down her fingertips. Beside her, on a bench inside the boat, Jacob slept. He hadn't woken during the entire incident with their captor, which wasn't normal. His breathing was also shallow. It terrified her.

Her gaze swung to the man driving the vessel. Alex Sheffield. His clothes were soaked from the rain, and yet some animal hair still clung to the fabric. Anger flooded Claire's veins. "What did you drug my son with?"

He smirked. "Don't worry, Sheriff. He'll be fine."

Jacob didn't look fine. His complexion was pale, his freckles standing out in sharp relief. Claire twisted her hands more, attempting once again to break the zip ties, but it was no use. They were industrial strength.

Her gaze swept the cabin. She needed something sharp to cut the bonds with. Beyond the windshield, the lake shore whizzed past. Claire's stomach bounced with each bump along the choppy waters. "Whatever you're planning, it won't work. Every law enforcement officer in the state will be looking for us."

Gavin would send help. Tears pricked Claire's eyes as she thought of her brave Texas Ranger. By now, he would've discovered she was missing. Along with Jacob. She couldn't imagine the depths of his worry and fear. It threatened to overwhelm the last bit of emotional control she was clinging to.

Don't think about it. There wasn't time. Her focus

needed to be on saving Jacob. As long as there was breath in her body, there was hope they could get out of this alive.

Alex's smirk widened. "I certainly hope everyone will look for you. How else can I frame Xavier for the murders?"

Claire's mind whirled as she struggled to put the pieces together. In Maribelle's cabin, Xavier had been insisting that someone was after him. Making it look like he'd done things he hadn't. He'd disappeared to find out who.

It was a member of his own group. Alex had attempted to take control of the Chosen once before. This was his opportunity to get rid of Xavier once and for all. She swallowed hard. "You killed Stephanie? And Faye?"

"Faye was collateral damage. She shouldn't have involved herself in matters that weren't her concern." His expression hardened. "As for Stephanie...she betrayed me. I loved her. I would've given her the world, but she decided our relationship was over. She was going to marry Ian. I couldn't let that happen."

They were trapped with a cold-blooded killer. Dread slithered through Claire like sludge. Alex wouldn't hesitate to hurt—even murder—Jacob. He had no conscience. Her gaze swept the sparse cabin again, searching desperately for anything to use as a weapon. She wouldn't let him hurt her son. "Where did you get the boat, Alex?"

It didn't belong to him. His family didn't own one. Alex passed her a quick glance. "I have friends in high places, Sheriff. I didn't start this without knowing I'd be protected if things went south."

So he wasn't working alone. That explained why he'd come after her. Alex didn't have the ability to pick a new sheriff, but whoever his partner was, did. Sweat beaded down Claire back. She had to figure out a way to over-power her kidnapper.

Alex lowered the boat's speed, bringing them closer to shore. The boat's rocking increased. Claire tumbled off the bench. She landed on the floor in a heap, crying out as Jacob's small form landed on her swollen knee. Her little boy didn't stir.

She wrangled herself into a sitting position. Jacob's breathing was still shallow but steady. Claire took some small comfort from that. She closed her eyes, folding herself over her son's small form. *Please, God, give me strength. Help me get through this. Watch over Jacob and keep him safe. He's just a little boy.*

The prayer centered her. She opened her eyes. A piece of twisted metal glinted on the floor nearby. Drawers used for storage were built into the bench she'd fallen from. A handle had recently been replaced. It was newer than the rest. The old one must've broken because a sliver was left behind.

Was it strong enough to cut the zip tie with? Maybe. Claire glanced at Alex, but his focus was on driving the boat. She twisted her body, wincing against the pain, and snagged the jagged piece of metal from the carpet. Twisting it in her fingers, she used the jagged end to slice at the zip ties. It was slow going.

"We're here." Alex killed the engine. He hauled Jacob back onto the bench with rough movements.

"Don't hurt him." Fury blinded her as she struggled to gain leverage into a standing position, even with her hands tied behind her back. The zip ties were weaker, but she still couldn't break them. "He's just a child. He has nothing to do with this."

Alex ignored her, grasping Claire's arm with a bruising grip. He roughly pulled her into a standing position. Pain shot through her swollen knee and she cried out. The jagged piece of metal tumbled from her fingers. Alex began dragging her to the door. "Let's go."

Suddenly, she realized he intended to separate her from Jacob. She tried to break his hold. "I'm not going anywhere without Jacob."

Alex tightened his grip and shoved a gun into her side. "Stop." His foul breath washed across her cheek, his dark eyes cold and flat. Evil. "If you do as I tell you, then Jacob will be left alive someplace safe where he'll be found. Fight me, and I'll kill him."

Claire's knees went weak. Alex meant every word. Her only option was to buy time, either until help arrived or until there was an opening to fight back.

Within moments, they were on shore. The frigid air cooled Claire's overheated skin. The rain had finally stopped, the cloud cover dissipating enough to allow beams of moonlight through. It streamed over the trees. This section of the lake was familiar. Xavier's land.

A man stood at the end of the dock. Mayor Patrick Scott. He wore a designer raincoat, his mouth twisted into a hard-edged sneer. Claire wasn't shocked by his presence. She'd been wrong about his accomplice—he'd paid Alex the $100,000 to kill Stephanie—but right about everything else. He'd had Stephanie murdered to prevent her from marrying his son. Faye's search for the missing woman threatened to expose their secret, and the mayor had killed her. Everything else that followed was part of a cleanup to keep their secrets buried. Including the threats against Claire.

Now the two men were making a desperate attempt to frame Xavier for everything. They didn't know the man was already in police custody.

Patrick's glare swept over Claire before landing on Alex. "You're late."

"There were some delays." Alex shoved Claire and her feet stumbled over each other. Her body crashed to the ground with enough force to knock the air from her lungs. The zip ties around her wrist broke. Before she had time to react, the sharp point of Patrick's boot landed in her stomach. Pain exploded through her body. Claire doubled over.

Patrick leaned down. "You've caused me a lot of trouble, Sheriff. I warned you to stay out of my way."

She sucked in a shallow breath. Spots danced in front of her vision. Patrick grabbed a fistful of her hair and yanked until she was looking him in the face. Fire raced along her scalp and the pain exacerbated her body's need for air.

He sneered. Menace dilated his pupils. "Shooting you is going to make me very happy."

Patrick released her and Claire tumbled back to the ground. Her hands were free, but her muscles wouldn't coordinate. The pain was overwhelming. Every breath sent burning through her chest. She felt as weak as a newborn kitten as Alex hauled her once again to her feet. He handed Patrick two handguns. "The Glock is hers. Make sure you dispose of it."

"I don't need you to tell me what to do," Patrick snapped. "Don't forget who's in charge. Let's get this over with."

Alex half-dragged, half-carried Claire behind the mayor toward the tree line. He deposited her next to a fallen pine. Leaves and pine needles cushioned her fall this time. Her mind whirled. She was an experienced law enforcement officer, but no amount of training had prepared her to take on two armed men with nothing but her bare hands.

She couldn't run. Jacob was still on the boat. He needed medical attention, and the only way to get to him was through her attackers. She had to fight. But how? Darkness pressed in around her. The boat bobbed on the black surface of the lake. There were no signs of anyone else nearby. Gavin and the rest of the law enforcement officers had to be looking for her by now, but Xavier's property wasn't the first place they'd go.

A jagged stick from the fallen log was in front of her. Claire wrapped her fingers around it. The bark cut into the tender flesh of her palm. The crude weapon wasn't much, but it was something. She sucked in a deeper breath, forcing herself to ignore the ache in her chest.

Patrick's phone beeped with an incoming message. He glanced at his smart watch. The glow cast stark shadows on his face. His muscles tightened.

"What is it?" Alex asked.

"An update from the Fulton County Sheriff's Department. Xavier's been arrested. He was taken into custody twenty minutes ago." Patrick raised a gun, pointing it at Claire. "That changes things."

He whirled and fired. Alex stumbled back as blood bloomed on his shirt. He collapsed into a heap, like a puppet whose strings had been cut. Horror and disgust churned Claire's stomach. She gripped the stick tighter in hand.

Patrick tossed her a smile. "You see, Claire. You never stood a chance against me. I'm smarter than anyone knows and I plan for every contingency." He lifted the gun in his hand. It was her service weapon. "You'll die, but at least you'll go out a hero. Killed while shooting your kidnapper."

Claire shifted her body weight in preparation to attack. She needed to edge closer. "It was your idea to kill Stephanie, wasn't it? You convinced Alex to do it."

"He didn't need much convincing. He was angry with Stephanie. I just provided a way for him to solve the problem." He smirked. "The money helped, of course."

"You didn't plan on Faye looking for Stephanie two years after she disappeared."

"I knew to keep my eye on her." He tucked her service weapon into his pocket and removed the second gun. "I heard rumblings around town and asked Alex to meet with Faye at the bakery. Like most people in town, she believed Alex had turned over a new leaf and put aside his criminal ways. She thought he cared about Stephanie as much as she did."

Faye had trusted Alex. That one mistake led to her death. Claire's mind filled in the blanks from what she knew about the case. "Faye believed Ian was involved in Stephanie's disappearance."

Patrick nodded. "I couldn't have that. I ordered Alex to eliminate her."

His tone was callous. Claire's body shook with rage, even as she slid toward the mayor. One hand gripped the stick. With the other, she grabbed a handful of dirt. "Alex sliced her tire and shot her in cold blood. And the private detective she hired."

"Yes. Most of the threats against you were him, too. I was the brains, but he was the muscle." Patrick pointed the gun at her. "He messed up quite a few times, but it worked out in the end. You've caused me a great deal of grief. Like I said, I'm going to enjoy shooting you."

Now! She flung the dirt in his face and the mayor yelped as it hit his eyes. He stumbled back and Claire swiped out with one leg to knock him off his feet. He hit the ground with a thud but held on to his weapon. She beat him with the stick. He rolled to get away from her. She kept up the assault, the pain in her chest making it hard to breathe, the throbbing in her leg slowing her down.

Claire attempted to restrain his hand with the weapon. She jabbed her elbow into his neck. He punched. Stars exploded in her head as his fist collided with her cheek. She fell back. Patrick followed the hit with another. Her body went limp.

He rose from the ground, like a horrific goblin from a scary movie. Blood dripped from his busted lip. Dirt and pine needles coated his clothes. Breathing heavily, Patrick lifted his weapon. Inside her head, Claire was screaming for her muscles to move, but they refused.

A shadow shifted behind the mayor. "Drop it."

Gavin's voice was an answer to a heartfelt prayer. The clouds parted and a beam of moonlight reflected off the gun held to the back of the mayor's head. She followed the arm holding it, lifted her gaze to the ranger's fierce expression. Claire's heart soared. She didn't know how Gavin had found her in time, but he had.

Ryker came into view, his weapon also drawn. "It's over. Drop the gun."

Claire held her breath. There was a chance Patrick would still decide to pull the trigger. She could see the war waging inside him. Finally, resignation seeped into his eyes. Patrick released his fingers, and the weapon dropped to the ground.

Claire kicked it away with her foot. Ryker moved in, grabbed the mayor by the back of the neck, and forced him to the ground. Gavin didn't shift his weapon away until the killer was handcuffed. Then he raced to Claire's side. Blood coated his shirt and his complexion was pale, but he was alive.

"Where are you hurt?" Gavin's hands ran over her face, smoothing away the strands of hair from her temple.

The fear and concern in his eyes twisted her insides. She wanted to dive into his embrace and never let go, but now wasn't the time.

Claire grabbed his arm. "Forget about me. Jacob's on the boat. Alex drugged him, but I don't know with what—"

Gavin raced for the vessel. He disappeared inside the cabin and came out moments later, cradling Jacob in his strong arms. Claire's heart tore at the look of anguish on Gavin's face. She struggled to her feet. "No, no, please no."

"He's okay, Claire." Gavin closed the distance between them. "He's waking up."

Relief rippled through her, threatening to weaken her knees and send her back to the ground. Tears ran down her face as she pressed a hand to her son's cheek. Jacob's eyes opened, his sleepy gaze fixing on her face. "Hi, Mommy."

She showered him with kisses. *Thank you, God, thank you.*

Gavin wrapped his arm around her, tucking her close. Tears shimmered in his eyes. He brushed his lips across hers. "I love you, Claire."

The world stopped, stealing Claire's breath. There was no denying the truth. Her heart belonged to Gavin and always would. Claire met his gaze before returning his kiss. "I love you too."

NINETEEN

Six months later

Gavin shrugged on his suit jacket and ran a hand down his tie. Nerves jittered his stomach. There were only twenty minutes until he had to be at the altar. The box with the wedding rings bulged against his leg. He pulled it out of his pocket and turned to Ryker, his best man. "Guard these with your life."

Ryker plucked the box from Gavin's hand. "I don't think it'll come to that. Unless you know of some other murderous criminals threatening you or Claire...I mean, I'm still recovering from last year. There's no way I'm helping you out again."

Gavin barked out a laugh. He gave his friend a gentle shove. "You barely did anything. I'm the one who was shot."

"The doctor called it a flesh wound. Thirty stitches

and you were good as new. Face it, Gavin. I drove that boat like a pro to Xavier's property, sliding it right up to the shore, so you could race in there and save Claire. We both know who the actual hero is."

He scoffed, buttoning his suit jacket. "You only knew where to go because I told you. If I hadn't overheard Xavier talk about being framed, you'd still be in that boat, wandering around looking for Claire."

Ryker raised a hand, his grin widening. "Okay, okay, you win. This time."

They both laughed. The humor was dark, especially for Gavin's wedding day, but there wasn't any way to escape how he and Claire had fallen in love. Or how close they'd come to losing each other.

Patrick Scott had been convicted and would spend the rest of his life in prison. His obsessive need to control Ian's life drove him to murder. His accomplice, Alex, died from his injuries. Neither man would ever harm Claire, or anyone else, again. For that, Gavin was grateful.

Xavier was also in prison. His arrest had led to the Chosen being dismantled. The survivalist group had been running a major drug operation for years. Maribelle still lived in Fulton County. She'd gotten medical care for her heart condition and her health stabilized. Claire and Gavin visited her from time to time. Ian moved several states away to start his life over.

Ryker opened the ring box. He whistled. "I can't believe you're taking the plunge. I was sure you'd stay single forever."

"So did I. God had other plans." Gavin's mouth quirked. "Watch out. You may be next."

Ryker snorted. "Not a chance. I have no interest in marriage, kids, or a white picket fence." He clapped a hand on Gavin's back. "But I'm happy for you, man. Truly. You've got something special with Claire."

Yes, he did. Over the last six months, they'd fallen more and more in love. Each day Gavin spent with her and Jacob was a blessing. He couldn't wait to start their lives together.

"Gavin, Gavin, Gavin."

The thundering sound of footsteps accompanied the repeated shouting of his name. Gavin turned as Jacob hurtled into the room. The little boy slid to a stop seconds from crashing into a couch. He grinned, eyes sparkling with happiness. "I'm ready!"

He looked adorable in a suit and bow tie. Gavin was tempted to ruffle the little boy's hair, but it was obvious someone—probably his grandmother—had attempted to tame the unruly curls. Instead, he offered his hand for a high five. "You look great, buddy."

Jacob smacked his palm. Then his face grew serious. "There's something I need to ask you."

"Sure thing." Gavin dropped to one knee, so they were at eye level. "What is it?"

"Today, you're marrying my mom, right? And that means we're going to be a family."

"Yep, that's right."

Jacob's gaze dropped to his patent leather shoes. His

mouth screwed up with concern. "So...would it be okay if I called you Dad?"

Gavin's chest squeezed tight. He and Claire had already discussed this possibility months ago. Gavin knew she was okay with it, and he'd hoped one day, Jacob would see him as a father figure. But he hadn't expected it to happen now.

A lump formed in the back of Gavin's throat and it took genuine effort to swallow it down. "I would love that, Jacob."

Pure joy erupted on the little boy's face. He tossed his arms around Gavin's neck and hugged him. The move was exuberant enough to nearly knock them off-balance. Jacob giggled.

Gavin tickled him, causing more peals of laughter. Then he straightened Jacob's suit jacket. "Okay, let's not mess up our clothes before the service." He winked. "There's plenty of time to do that at the reception."

"We're going to have cake! Mommy says it's chocolate. That's my favorite."

"I know. We picked it with you in mind."

A knock on the doorframe interrupted their conversation. Claire's father, Daniel, stood in the doorway. His suit was pressed and beard neatly trimmed. In one hand, he held a leash. Gavin's dog, Lucky, greeted the room with a bark. Jacob raced to his side and petted the Labrador's head. The two were best buddies and had been since the day Gavin adopted Lucky from the animal shelter last year. In the end, the puppy with the white spot on his head had stolen his heart. Gavin couldn't resist bringing him home.

It was the beginning of a new life. One in which Gavin left the old hurts in the past and let himself chase his dreams—all of them.

"Time to go," Daniel announced. He locked eyes with Gavin. "You ready?"

"Absolutely." Wild horses couldn't keep him away.

The church was filled with summer flowers. Pews overflowed with guests. All the members of Company A were there. Lieutenant Rodriguez with her family, Grady and Tara, Luke and Megan, Weston and Avery, Bennett and Emilia.

Gavin considered them all close friends. The couples had been supportive of his relationship with Claire from the word go, and their loving relationships were inspiring. He couldn't believe he'd ever worried about having a family alongside his Texas Ranger career.

Ryker joined him at the altar. The music started and the rear doors opened. Jacob marched down the aisle, one hand gripping Lucky's leash, a broad smile on his face. The guests laughed at the cuteness overload. Claire's mother, seated in the front row, dabbed at her eyes with a tissue.

Jacob was supposed to take his seat next to his grand-mother but deviated from the course to climb the steps of the altar. He grinned up at Gavin and then turned to stand with him. Lucky sat, obediently. Chuckles and claps came from the audience.

Ryker patted Jacob's shoulder. "Smart move, kid."

It was a brilliant move. Gavin couldn't imagine Jacob being anywhere else other than at his side. It felt like his chest would explode with happiness and love. He bent down to whisper in Jacob's ear. "Your mom comes out next."

"I know."

The music changed. Gavin's gaze shot to the rear of the church, his heart in his throat.

Claire appeared at the end of the aisle on her father's arm. The wedding dress flowed over her curves in layers of soft fabric. Her hair was intricately curled and decorated with small flowers. She carried a matching bouquet. The ribbon wrapped around the flowers was the same shade as her eyes. Each step Claire took forward made Gavin's heart beat faster. He'd never seen a more beautiful sight.

Their gazes locked. Time stood still as the church and everyone else faded away. Gavin saw his future in Claire's eyes. She was his everything. The love between them would last for a lifetime, the vows they were about to take, promises neither would break.

He placed a hand on Jacob's shoulder as emotion threatened to unravel him. God had answered his prayers. It was all here, in this church. Love. Friends. A family. Even a dog named Lucky.

ALSO BY LYNN SHANNON

Texas Ranger Heroes Series

Ranger Protection

Ranger Redemption

Ranger Courage

Ranger Faith

Ranger Honor

Triumph Over Adversity Series

Calculated Risk

Critical Error

Would you like to know when my next book is released? Or when my novels go on sale? It's easy. Subscribe to my newsletter at www.lynnshannon.com and all of the info will come straight to your inbox!

Reviews help readers find books. Please consider leaving a review at your favorite place of purchase or anywhere you discover new books. Thank you.

Printed in Great Britain
by Amazon

19942861R00130